Sha

of the

Werewolf

Magnus Hansen

This is a work of fiction. Names, characters, organizations, places, events, and incidents are either products of the author's imagination or are used fictitiously.

Cover design from: depositphotos

Chapter 1

Birka - a town on the east coast of Sweden, 950AD

"We live on a placid island of ignorance in the midst of black seas of infinity, and it was not meant that we should voyage far."

-H.P. Lovecraft, The Call of Cthulhu

"You arrived at a bad time, my friend."

Cathal steadied himself on the swaying docks, as rough waves crashed against the rotted pilings. "How so?" he asked.

The old fisherman exhaled loudly, then said, "People are afraid, so they aren't hiring.

The only job you're going to find around here is chopping wood at the lumber camp." He set down the bucket of fish he was carrying and rubbed his calloused hands.

"What about the other industries?"

Squinting his eyes, the old Norseman cocked his head to the side, sizing up the new arrival. "You *are* new around here. Haven't even heard the rumors yet, I take it?"

Shaking his head, Cathal said, "No. Can't say that I have."

Letting out a grunt as he bent down to retrieve his bucket, the fisherman said, "Follow me to the market, and I'll let you in on a bit of local gossip."

Cathal continued to stroll down the creaking dock, beside the old man. He was hoping to get a job at the infirmary, but he was willing to accept any type of employment, if the money was right.

"The town of Birka is in a bit of a mess these days," said the fisherman.

Cathal found the long, confident stride of the Norseman difficult to keep up with. "Why is that?" he asked.

"It's the damn foreigners. No offense, mind you. Too many migrants have been coming to our shores. So many, they outnumber the Norsemen. There's Slavs and Goths and Turks-"

"I'm surprised the Turks would come this far north," interrupted Cathal.

The old fisherman gave the new arrival a sideways glance as he switched the heavy bucket to his other hand. "The Turks go wherever there's money to be made, but I suppose that could be said of all the men here. The Turks have taken over the reindeer herding camps. The Slavs have taken over the lumber camps. The Norsemen still hold onto the mining and fishing industries. It's the herding and lumber operations where men are being murdered, so the Norsemen don't mind too much."

"What? Are there any suspects?"

Instead of answering, the fisherman stopped in front of one of the bustling market shops alongside the shore and started to barter with the shopkeeper. After a few moments of intense arguing, the Norseman received three silver coins for the bucket of fish. He nodded as he placed the coins into an old leather pouch tied to his belt. "What were we talking about?" he finally asked.

With an incredulous look, Cathal said, "The murders..."

"Ah, right. The murders. Follow me to the tavern and I'll tell you all about it. The first round is on me," he said, tapping his coin pouch with his fingers.

Cathal let out a heavy sigh. What choice did he have? He just arrived in Birka. He had no connections, and his own coin pouch was nearly empty. Quiet and sullen, he once again fell in step with the Norseman, as they ambled over the rutted, muddy road. A few minutes later they found themselves seated in a smoky tavern filled with dangerous looking men.

The old fisherman leaned forward in his chair and said, "About a year ago, wolves started to attack the loggers and reindeer herders to the north. In the beginning, there were only one or two attacks per month, but recently, the attacks have become more frequent, more deadly. The Turks and Slavs are blaming the Norsemen, saying the wolves are being unnaturally aggressive, as if they were trained to kill. It's true the Norsemen want the migrants out. Another foreigner murdered in the woods is a cause for celebration, as far as they're concerned. But the foreigners are too firmly entrenched. If they leave now, the entire economy of Birka would collapse."

"Trained wolves?" asked Cathal, crinkling his brow.

The fisherman grunted and rapped his knuckles on the table. "It's nonsense, of course. Both the Turks and the Slavs are superstitious fools. They'd accuse their own mothers if it meant another silver coin in their pockets. No, the reindeer herders and woodcutters simply have the misfortune of encroaching on the territory of a large wolf pack. Birka is situated on a small island on the eastern edge of the mainland. The wolves have nowhere else to go; they're simply defending their territory."

A large serving girl with troubled eyes clopped over to the table and set two cups of mead in front of them. The fisherman pushed a coin in her direction and waved her off. He then took a smoking pipe that was wedged in his belt and held it up to the light. Seemingly satisfied, he stuck one end of the pipe in his mouth, grabbed a candle that was laying on the table, and lit the pipe. He coughed a few times as he drew smoke, then spat a glob of phlegm on the floor.

Cathal quietly observed the man as he sipped his cup of mead. "About that job..."

"Right! Well, you won't be able to find work as a fisherman, I can tell you that. If you're not a Norseman like me, no one will hire you. Same goes for working in the copper mines. The only place you'll be able to find employment is at the logging camp."

"I can chop wood."

The Norseman almost choked on his pipe. "Hmm, yes. Glad to hear it." He then brought up his cup and took a sip of mead. His eyes were intently studying Cathal. "There's a reason why they need new workers. Lately, one or two woodcutters have died every week in the forest, and the ones who survive the attacks get the frothing disease."

"Frothing disease?"

"Aye. The infirmary is full of the poor wretches. The wolves carry some kind of disease that, once a man is bitten, brings about a fever. After a couple of days, the victims start vomiting and frothing at the mouth. A few days after that, they're dead."

"I have heard of this disease," said Cathal, shaking his head. "There's no cure for it."

"Aye."

During the break in conversation, Cathal took the opportunity to study the men in the tavern. It was easy to distinguish the Norsemen – they were tall and robust, of fair hair and full beard. The Slavs were of a darker complexion – black hair and angular faces. The Turks were the most curious – they had dark eyes, close-cropped beards and olive skin. All those men had endured harsh, brutal lives. Numerous scars covered their exposed skin. No matter the race, their demeanor seemed to match their rough countenance.

Through the crowded room, Cathal continued to study the faces of those beastly men. They seemed deeply troubled; their conversations muted. They cast furtive glances amongst themselves. It was then that his eyes settled upon a Slavic man who was looking intently at him. Startled, Cathal looked down at his drink.

"Tomorrow you get a job, yes?" asked the fisherman, as he slapped his heavy, calloused hand on Cathal's shoulder.

Pursing his lips, Cathal said, "You sure I can't get a job fishing? Or working on the docks?"

"I'm afraid not. In this town, Norsemen only hire Norsemen. If I were you, I'd resign myself to getting a job at the logging camp. Its run by the Slavs, but at least they're more trustworthy than the Turks. Though you're still going to need to watch your back – if the wolves don't get you, those Slavic criminals will. They're little better than common vagabonds."

"I have some experience with medicine. Perhaps the infirmary could use a new doctor?"

The fisherman shook his head. "The infirmary is run by a völva. Unless you've pledged your allegiance to the Norse gods, you won't find any work there. Besides, medicine is for women."

"Harrumph!" grumbled Cathal, looking at the bottom of his empty cup.

* * * * * * *

Cathal woke to the stinging kick of a leather boot. He'd spent the night at the workman's camp — a temporary shelter used to house migrant workers. He could hear men grumble and complain in a mixture of foreign languages, as they put on their clothes and prepared themselves for another day of hard labor.

After pulling on his boots, Cathal walked over to the campfire and asked a passerby where the logging camp was located. The man, a Slav by the look of him, raised his arm and pointed to the north. "About a half mile up the trail," he said with a lazy yawn, before continuing on his way.

Looking around, Cathal wondered where the workers acquired their rations. Was food provided, or was it their responsibility to provide for themselves? In his travels, he noticed that each culture had different notions about such matters. He unconsciously pinched the coin pouch that was tied to his belt...only a few coins left; enough for a few days of sustenance, and little else.

"Heading up to the logging camp?" asked a voice from behind him.

Cathal swung his head around and was surprised to find a slender Irishman standing next to a very large wolfhound. "Yes. It's to the north, right?"

"Aye, follow us. The man who runs the logging camp doesn't take kindly to slackers. I hope you're ready for a hard day's work."

"Hard work never bothered me," remarked Cathal, falling into step beside the man. The wolfhound happily followed them. "That's some animal you've got there."

"Old Biter is the only reason I got a job at the lumber camp. The Slavs like to hire their own, but the wolves have been killing off workers faster than they can refill the positions. Once they saw the size of Biter, they hired me on the spot."

"That's an interesting name for a dog."

"Ha! I suppose it is. Her real name is Amber, and she's a real sweetheart. But around these types of people, you need to act tough. My name is Faolan, by the way."

"Cathal. Nice to meet you."

They walked up a leaf-covered trail. Overhead, the morning sun began to peek behind the branches of towering oak trees, which cast looming shadows on the path before them. Cathal could smell freshly cut timber.

"I think there's a position available, but don't be surprised if they place you on the northern perimeter, close to where the wolf attacks have been taking place."

"Have the attacks really been that bad?" asked Cathal.

To this, Faolan snorted so hard, that a string of snot shot out of his crooked nose and landed on his unkempt beard. "Worse!" he said, absently dabbing at his beard with the cuff of his sleeve. "They're intelligent bastards. Sometimes I'll catch a glimpse of them far off in the treeline, then a moment later they're gone. Last week I saw a pack of a half-dozen wolves chasing a man to the edge of the river.

The man jumped into the water and swam to the far shore, only to be ambushed by a dozen wolves on the other side!"

Cathal's eyes grew wide. "That's unbelievable."

"Believe it. You'll probably be getting that man's old job."

Try as he might, it was difficult for Cathal to not feel a little apprehensive.

"Ah, don't worry about it." Faolan slapped him on the back. "Just stick with me and old Biter, and you'll be safe enough. There's one thing you should know before you meet the foreman. Everyone in Birka is borderline racist, and the murders aren't helping matters. The Slavs are actually accusing the Norsemen of the attacks, saying the wolves are trained to hunt and kill foreigners."

"I've heard. Why would they say that?"

"Once you see those wolves in action, you'll understand. They act with an unnatural intelligence. I picked up a few words of Slavic since I've been working here, and from what I understand, the Slavs have seen a man walking amongst the wolves."

Cathal furrowed his brow and gave his companion a sidelong glance. "That's ridiculous."

Shaking his head, Faolan said, "Doesn't matter if it sounds ridiculous or not – they believe it."

As they came to a clearing in the woods, Cathal could see a group of men sitting around a low-burning campfire, warming themselves. Almost as one, they turned and looked at the new arrivals with dark, brooding eyes. When they saw that it was Faolan, his hound, and a rather plain-looking foreigner, they turned back around and continued to speak amongst themselves.

"Who's in charge?" whispered Cathal.

Faolan nodded towards a small wooden cabin, just beyond the campfire. "Domyan is the man who runs this camp. You'll want to speak to him or his sister, Danika."

As Faolan and his wolfhound sat by the fire, Cathal walked towards the cabin with tentative steps. If he couldn't get a job here as a woodcutter, he could try his hand at reindeer herding, but that idea didn't appeal to him. He would rather not be up to his knees in deer guts all day long.

After knocking on the door, Cathal looked back over his shoulder, towards the group of men that were lounging around the campfire. Out of the dozen or so men that were quietly conversing, most were Slavs, a few were of Turkish descent, and Faolan. Biter walked around the campfire, accepting pets and greetings from the rough-looking men.

The door creaked open and a tall, rather ominous looking Slavic man stepped out. He had straight black hair that framed his strong, angular face. Instead of a traditional beard, the man wore long sideburns that traveled halfway down his scarred jawline. He glanced at the men sitting by the campfire, then casually looked at Cathal with a raised eyebrow. Rubbing his chin, he cocked his head and said, "You look familiar... Ah, yes. I remember you from the tavern last night."

Cathal's eyes slightly widened. *That* was the man he'd locked eyes with last night at the tavern!

"I suppose you're here for a job," said Domyan, as he cleared his throat and spat a giant glob of phlegm to the ground. "You only need two requirements to work here. One – you work hard. And two – you're not a Norseman. So, what say you? You're not a Norseman, are you?"

"Irish. Pleased to meet you." Cathal offered his hand in greeting.

Domyan looked at the offered hand with a mixture of boredom and amusement. He then flashed a sinister smile and slapped Cathal on the shoulder, ignoring his hand. "Another Irishman, eh? You'll be working on the northern perimeter today. Faolan will show you the way." He then scratched his lower back and yawned.

The men around the campfire cast furtive glances at Domyan. Seeing their apprehension, the foreman picked up a large stone from the ground and threw it at the campfire, causing a huge plum of fire and sparks to shower over the laborers. "Well, daylight's burning," yelled Domyan. "Get to work!"

Scrambling to grab their axes, the workers quickly stepped towards their assigned areas of the lumber camp. The foreman watched the workers with narrowed eyes, looking for any sign of idleness. Then, with a bored grunt, he turned around, walked back into his cabin, and slammed the door shut.

Cathal was left standing there, alone. A whistle from the northern woodline pulled him from his contemplations.

"Grab an ax from the tool shed and follow me," said Faolan. "And pray we don't see any wolves today."

Chapter 2

"Have you ever worked as a woodcutter?" asked Faolan.

The two men stood at the northern edge of the lumber camp, while Biter happily loped off in search of rabbits. The morning sun shown brightly overhead, casting a multitude of swaying shadows upon the forest floor. The faint sound of chopping could be heard in the distance.

"I've chopped down trees," replied Cathal.

"That's not what I asked." Faolan turned around and pointed at a group of trees to his left. "I'm sure you've noticed the birch trees around here. Birka is located on the island of Björkö, which literally means 'birch island'. Birch is a fine wood, but its real value lies in the bark. They make tar from the bark, which Norsemen use to seal their longships. The Norsemen also have a drink they make from birch sap – after it's fermented, the stuff has a real kick!"

"I've had that drink more than once," admitted Cathal.

With a laugh, Faolan said, "Spoken like a true Irishman." He then pointed to another cluster of trees. "Over there you can see a few spruce and pine trees. The wood on those trees is mostly used for furniture – outside exposure will cause the wood to rot, after a time." He then pointed to one last group of trees. "And of course, we use the oak trees for everything else – building longships, cabins, ax-handles, just about anything you can think of. That's the type of tree we're mostly interested in, but I'll have you start with chopping down the smaller birch trees. After a few days, I'll show you how we take down the bigger oaks."

"I appreciate your help," said Cathal, as he hefted his two-handed ax and began to chop away at one of the birch trees.

Faolan watched him for a few moments, then walked towards another group of trees, mumbling under his breath, "Where did that damn dog run off to?"

Cathal kept his mind on the task at hand. After a time, he fell into a comfortable rhythm. Despite the physical exertion required, chopping wood was boring, mindless work. To compensate, his mind often wandered, thinking about trivialities. Was there a daily quota? When were they going to pay him? Could the foreman be trusted?

During his contemplations, he would often look up and wearily gaze into the forest. Wolves were out there somewhere, watching. Waiting. He shook his head and continued on. Several times an hour, he would hear another tree in the distance fall to the ground. At midday, he heard a horn sound off in the distance. Time for lunch.

Looking down at his hands, Cathal could already see blisters forming. He leaned his ax against the birch tree and proceeded to pop a few blisters, wincing as the clear fluid streamed down his hand.

As he wiped his hands on his trousers, he saw movement from the corner of his eye. He quickly glanced to his left and right. Nothing. The foreman then blew the horn a second time.

Cathal picked up his ax and slowly walked back to the main camp, cautiously looking over his shoulder every few moments. He could smell the pine logs of the campfire burning just up ahead. Hiking down the last stretch of trail, he saw Faolan and the rest of the woodcutters just up ahead. Biter ran towards him with a big grin on his furry snout.

"I see you found Biter," said Cathal.

"Aye. She likes to wander off. Come get some food, before it's all gone." Faolan pointed to a spit over the campfire.

"Smells good," noted Cathal. "What are we eating?"

With a mouth full of food, Faolan said, "Reindeer. Always reindeer."

This brought a few grunts of laughter from the Slavic men. Then one fellow with a raspy voice said, "Not always. Sometimes we eat wolf."

Cathal gave the man an apprehensive glance. He then cut a few strips of meat from the reindeer and sat down next to Faolan. Hungry beyond measure, he eagerly dug into his plate of food.

"Let me see your hands," asked Faolan.

Resting the plate of food on his knees, Cathal raised his hands, palms up, revealing multiple blisters and contusions.

"Ah, hell. I forgot to tell you to wrap your hands. That's going to hurt tomorrow."

"Huh. Not just tomorrow." Cathal shrugged his shoulders and continued to eat. As he ate, he stole a few glances at the other men, curious as to who he was working with. Most of the men were of Slavic descent, with black or brown hair and angular features. They were dangerous looking men – their bodies and faces were crossed with multiple scars and abrasions. The three Turkish men look equally formidable, with piercing eyes and menacing dispositions.

Noticing his curiosity, one of the Slavic men, the one with the raspy voice, said, "You're an Englishman, eh?"

Cathal looked up from his plate. "Irish."

"Huh. What brings you all this way, *Englishman*?" said the man with the raspy voice.

Studying the Slavic man, Cathal could see that he had a long red scar across the entire front of his neck. From a noose, perhaps? "I'm just trying to earn enough coin for passage back to Ireland."

"And why did you leave your country in the first place?" asked the man.

"I'm a doctor, and there was money to be made with all the wars brewing to the south. I worked my way eastward through the Frankish kingdoms, until I found myself in a small town on the southern shores of the Baltic Sea. I waited for two months in that town for passage back to Ireland. During that time, only one Norse captain was going in that direction, and he wanted far too much money. I eventually found cheap passage to Birka."

"Huh," grunted the man. He coughed and winced, then he reached up and rubbed the front of his neck.

At that moment, the foreman stepped out of his cabin and walked towards the campfire. He said, "Never mind Mirko. He doesn't trust Englishmen *or* Irishmen. Hasn't trusted them since they strung him up for stealing horses. Isn't that right, Mirko?"

The man with the red scar grunted and kept his eyes on his plate.

"Let me see your hands," ordered Domyan. Once again, Cathal set down his plate and held up his hands. Domyan let out a long whistle and said, "That's what I like to see! Someone who knows how to work. You should have wrapped your hands."

"So I hear," replied Cathal, chagrined.

Domyan approached the spit and tore off a chunk of reindeer meat. Not bothering with a plate or utensils, he looked at the northern woodline as he chewed, making grunting noises every few moments.

Cathal noticed that the woodcutters seemed restless around the foreman. They quietly ate their lunch as Domyan paced around the campfire.

"You." Domyan pointed at one of the Turkish men.

The man slowly looked up with more than a little apprehension in his eyes.

"I want you at the northeastern edge of camp, where the alder trees are. We just received an order for alder wood."

Nodding slowly, the Turkish man set his eyes on his plate.

Domyan observed the man for a moment, deciding if he should say something more. He then grunted and threw his handful of reindeer meat into the campfire. With measured steps, he walked back to his cabin and slammed the door shut behind him.

With a crinkled brow, Cathal looked at Faolan, who kept his head down and offered a single warning glance. *Don't ask.*

After lunch, the men retrieved their axes and returned to work. Cathal struggled to keep up with Faolan, who was walking with purpose. Biter trotted alongside him, seemingly unconcerned.

"What was that all about?" asked Cathal.

Faolan let out a sharp exhale. "Domyan can tell when one of his loggers isn't pulling his weight. He puts them on the northern edge of camp, where all the wolf attacks have been taking place. That's why he placed you up north – you're new, and you need to prove yourself. If you work hard for a few weeks, he'll probably relocate you to another area. At least that's what he did for me."

"What did the Turkish man do?"

Shaking his head, Faolan said, "I have no idea. He works on the other side of camp. But it's no secret that Domyan favors his Slavs. Not one Slav has worked on the northern edge of camp in months."

"When was the last wolf attack?"

Faolan unconsciously peered into the woodline. He spoke in a low, conspiratorial tone, barely audible. "Last week the wolves brought down a Turkish man just to the northeast – the same place Domyan ordered that man to cut down the alder trees." Then, he pointed to the left, and in a louder voice, he said, "I'm stationed over there, to the west. Do you remember where those birch trees are?"

Cathal nodded.

"Good. If you see any trouble, just yell out a warning and run towards the south. They're not paying you to be brave." He then turned to his left and walked down a narrow trail, with Biter following happily behind him.

Cathal watched after him for a moment, then continued northward. As he walked, he mulled over his current prospects. He was convinced that staying as a logger would eventually get him killed. *This* was a job for desperate men, not a respectable doctor. He couldn't get a job working the copper mines, the infirmary, *or* the docks, simply because he was Irish. There was a chance he could get a job as a reindeer herder, but that job was just as dangerous as logging. He shook his head in agitation. He knew this assignment was going to be dangerous, but not *this* dangerous.

Up ahead, he could see the cluster of birch trees he was working on. To the left were the half-dozen logs he'd already cut down, neatly pruned of branches and stacked in an orderly pile. With a heavy sigh, he hefted his two-handed ax and started chopping. After three swings of the ax, he stopped and let out a weary chuckle. He was so caught up in tales of wolves, that he forgot to grab some rags to wrap his hands with. Cursing himself for a fool, he continued to chop away at the birch trees.

Several hours later, the sun was still hanging high in the sky. It was June, and the sun didn't set until late in the evening. *What time did they finish work?*

Cathal looked down at his hands and snorted. His palms were raw and bleeding, with the first few layers of skin peeled off. After work, he would need to go to the market and pick up a poultice for his wounds. A mixture of myrrh and calendula flower should do the trick, he surmised.

Cathal suddenly looked up from his hands, startled. *What was that?* A sound...off in the distance. Was someone yelling? He turned his head slightly to the left and right, trying to get a bearing on the faint noise.

There it was again! Someone yelling, coming closer. He gripped his ax with both hands and stood with his back against a cluster of trees. He intently scanned the forest around him. As he stood there apprehensively, he remembered Faolan's words: *They're not paying you to be brave.* A part of him wanted to break and run to the south, but he stood his ground, despite his misgivings.

He squinted his eyes as he saw movement in the woods up ahead. Peering closer, he could see a Turkish man running towards him, flailing his arms, screaming. Cathal took a tentative step backward. He then saw what the man was running from – three wolves, panting and smiling, enjoying the chase.

Chapter 3

He ran as if the flames of hell were licking at his feet. Every few strides, the Turk would turn around and wildly swing his ax, trying to keep the wolves at bay. The wolves would deftly leap to the side, avoiding his clumsy attacks. The beasts seemed to laugh and dance at his misfortune.

Though his instincts begged him to flee, Cathal instead broke into a dead run towards the man. He could see the Turk's eyes, wide with terror, pleading for help.

In a coordinated movement, one of the wolves attacked the man's left side. As the Turk swung his ax in defense, another wolf sneaked up to his right and sunk its teeth into the man's leg. Cathal could hear the snap of bone as the Turk fell forward and skidded to a stop, his arms and legs flailing in a cloud of dirt and leaves.

The wolves started to swarm on the man, biting and pulling. Their ears then stood erect, as Cathal let out a bloodcurdling scream and lunged at the closest predator.

Momentarily startled, the wolves deftly scampered away a few paces, then turned around. Deciding the odds were still in their favor, the savage animals crept forward as Cathal forcefully swung his ax in a menacing arc.

"Ya! Ya!" he screamed, as he swung his ax before him.

The wolves carefully kept out of range as they circled around to a flanking position, heads low to the ground and growling. Seeing an easy opportunity, one of the wolves turned its attention back towards the Turk. The wolf lunged at the man and received a kick to the snout for its efforts.

As the wolf let out a sharp cry and jumped back, Cathal saw an opening and swung his ax. The blade sunk into its neck with a satisfying thud. To his horror, Cathal saw another wolf lunge at his left side, as he tried desperately to pull his ax free from the twitching carcass.

At the last second, Cathal let go of the ax and held up his arms, shielding his face. Expecting to be barreled over by the wolf's charge, he was surprised to hear a yelp, as the wolf was knocked out of the air mid-leap by Biter! The wolfhound, easily fifty pounds heavier, pounced on the wolf and closed its jaws around its neck, snapping it cleanly. The two remaining wolves quickly turned around and tore into the woods, cutting their losses.

Cathal put his hands on his knees to steady himself. After a few heavy breaths, he stood up and retrieved his ax. He then walked over to Biter and patted her on the head. "Good girl," he whispered.

The Turkish man was holding onto his leg, screaming. The man's thigh bone was snapped in two, and was sticking out of his leg by several inches. The rest of his leg bent backwards at an unnatural angle.

Gripping his ax, Cathal once again looked desperately around him, ready for another attack. He then saw a shadow move in the far distance, close to where the wolves had fled. Squinting his eyes, he saw the shadow glide between two trees. It then seemed to peer back at him with intelligent eyes, then vanished.

That was no wolf, was all he could think.

After a few tentative moments, Cathal heard something crash through the woods behind him. Spinning around, he saw Faolan and several other men running towards him. With a sigh of relief, he dropped his ax and knelt down beside the injured Turk and started to tend to the man's wounds.

"What happened?" asked Faolan. His head swiveled around, scanning the woods around him. He was breathing heavily and perspiring. His eyes were wide and full of apprehension.

"What do you think happened?" retorted Cathal, grimacing as he tried unsuccessfully to jam the Turk's leg bone back into place. Blood spurted onto his face and chest in rhythmic pulses, as the doctor tried to stabilize his patient.

The Turk was screaming, trying to push Cathal away.

"Grab his arms and legs!" ordered Cathal. He held up his hands, shielding himself from the Turk's desperate blows.

Faolan quickly grabbed the Turk's arms, while the two Slavic men each grabbed a leg. The Turk was now gasping and crying. He was looking towards the sky for some invisible savior. His body then hung slack, as he fell into unconsciousness.

Cathal looked up and addressed the man who was holding the Turk's left leg. "Gently pull on his leg so I can fit the bone back in place. Quickly, before he wakes up."

The woodcutter gritted his teeth and turned his head away as he pulled back, sickened by the unnatural give in the man's leg. He gasped and clenched his eyes shut, then said, "Hurry."

Shifting his gaze to the south, Cathal could see Domyan slowly walking up the trail towards him. Shaking his head, he then looked down and set his mind to the task at hand. He clenched the Turk's thigh with his right hand, while pushing the bone back into place with his other hand.

After the bone popped into place, the Turk's eyes shot open and he let out a gasping scream; it was an eerie sound that had no breath behind it. He then fell back into unconsciousness.

With a deep breath, Cathal wiped his hands on his tunic, then motioned for the men to gently set down the Turk's arms and legs. "We'll need to make a splint or a cast," he said in a quiet voice. Then, looking at the pile of birch logs, he added, "Take your axes and scrape off as much bark from those birch logs as you can."

"Why?" asked Faolan.

"For a cast. It's an old trick. We'll soak the birch bark in water, until it gets soggy. Then we'll form the wet bark around the Turk's leg. As it hardens, it will form into a cast. It's as good as a splint – better, in my estimation."

Faolan and the two other loggers started to dutifully cut thin strips of bark off the birch logs.

"I also need someone to run to the infirmary and fetch a needle and thread. I need to sew the wound on his leg before we put on the cast."

By this time, Domyan was standing next to the unconscious body of the Turk. The foreman was chewing on a short twig and had a bored look in his eyes. Casting his gaze to the north, he said, "Just another day at the logging camp, eh?" He let out a low chuckle, then pointed at one of the woodcutters. "You. Run to the infirmary and get a needle and thread." He then knelt down, rested his arms on his knee, and said, "He's going to make it, then?"

"He should make it. Provided the wound doesn't get infected."

Nodding his head in an unconcerned manner, Domyan said, "Know of anyone else who needs a job?" He then laughed and slapped Cathal on the back. "Just kidding. You did a good job here. Didn't realize that I was getting a doctor as well as a woodcutter when I hired you."

"Well, you can thank the Norsemen – *they* don't hire outsiders."

Domyan stood up and spat the twig out of his mouth. "Thank you, Norsemen," he said to no one in particular, softly chuckling to himself. He then said, "Let me know if you need anything else." He then walked back to camp, hands clasped behind him, whistling an old Slavic tune as he went.

When the foreman was out of sight, Cathal shot a glance towards Faolan and said, "He seems in an unusually good mood."

Faolan shrugged his shoulders and said, "Domyan's temperament runs hot and cold. You never know what you're going to get."

About a half hour passed before the logger finally returned from the infirmary. He had a forlorn look in his eyes as he said, "The völva who works at the infirmary refuses to hand out medical supplies."

"What?" barked Cathal. "Why not?"

The Slavic man looked troubled. Finally, he scratched at his neck and said, "They don't like to waste medical supplies on foreigners."

Cathal looked at the man in disbelief. He then gritted his teeth and said, "We'll see about that!" Breaking into a run, he raced southward, towards Birka.

In a matter of minutes, Cathal ran past the logging camp, where Domyan was sitting by the campfire. The foreman raised his eyebrows as the doctor ran past him, not even slowing down to acknowledge his presence. Domyan then snorted, as he watched the doctor run into the distance.

Damned Northerners, thought Cathal, as he raced towards town. He was starting to perspire heavily under the hot sun. He slowed his pace to a jog as he reached the outer edge of town. A few of the villagers looked at him with mild curiosity as he hurried past.

He slowed to a walk as the infirmary finally came into sight. Taking deep breaths, he tried to steady himself before he opened the door. Angry accusations wouldn't help him acquire the medical supplies he needed, he reminded himself.

The infirmary was a longhouse set on the eastern edge of town. Shutters were propped open, letting out the acrid smell of diseased and dying men. As Cathal opened the door, the smell of septic miasma nearly overwhelmed him. It was a stark contrast to the crisp air of the logging camp.

Stepping inside, he noticed several rows of cots that lined the length of the longhouse. Nurses were busily walking about, administering to sick patients. The patients were all Norsemen, Cathal noted. Steeling his resolve, he walked towards one of the nurses and said, "I have a man who's suffered a broken leg at the logging camp. I need supplies."

The nurse gave him a guarded look, then pointed towards an old woman who was working at the far end of the infirmary. "Ask the völva," she said simply, then turned back to her duties.

Völva? thought Cathal. He knew of them – a völva was a Norse seeress who could predict the future and speak to the gods. Kings and chieftains often called upon their wisdom for guidance in matters of politics and war.

With tentative steps, he walked towards the old woman. As he stepped closer, the völva looked up and scowled. Cathal could only surmise it was because he was a migrant. "I have a man who is injured at the logging camp. I need a needle and thread."

The old woman turned away and did her best to ignore him. "I'll tell you the same thing I told the last man who bothered me with this nonsense. We're short on medical supplies, and can't afford to hand any out."

"Can't afford to hand any out? Or can't afford to hand any out to foreigners?" asked Cathal through clenched teeth.

The völva turned towards him with a look of disdain. Her wrinkled face was framed with auburn hair that was more gray then red. She peeled back her lips and said, "The recent wolf attacks have strained our supplies. We only hand out medical provisions in case of an emergency."

"This *is* an emergency!" he implored.

The old woman narrowed her eyes and coldly said, "An emergency for you, perhaps. Not for me."

Cathal simply stood there, dumbfounded. He then spun on his heel, while grumbling a curse under his breath, and stormed out of the infirmary. *Unbelievable...just unbelievable*, he thought to himself. He stood in front of the building, unsure of what to do, until he saw a fisherman walk down the road. The man was carrying a bucket of fish. Cathal's eyes slightly widened as an idea came to him.

Turning to his left, Cathal ran towards the docks. If he couldn't get a needle and thread from the infirmary, he could at least get a hook and fishing line from the fishermen at the docks! As he approached the shoreline, he asked several fishermen for aid.

The fishermen and dockworkers, all Norsemen, looked at him with indifferent eyes, then continued about their business, unconcerned.

Cathal looked around in desperation, when his eyes finally settled upon a familiar face – it was the old fisherman he'd met just yesterday! He was walking towards him and carrying a huge dead fish, slung over his shoulder.

As he trotted up to the man, the old fisherman waved with his free hand. "You get job as woodcutter, yes?" he asked.

Cathal held up his hands, displaying his blistered palms.

"Ah, you should have worn wraps," said the old man, shaking his head.

"That's what they tell me," answered Cathal, ruefully shaking his head. "I'm in a bit of a hurry. Do you know where I can get a hook and fishing line?"

The old man stopped in front of Cathal and furrowed his brow. "Yes, back in the boat. Here, hold this." He hefted the fish off his shoulder and handed it to Cathal, then walked back to the rickety fishing boat that was tethered at the end of the dock.

With a look of surprise, Cathal staggered under the weight of the fish. The cod must have weighed over eighty pounds! It was a slippery thing, too. He clenched his teeth and tried to engender an air of confidence, when in fact he struggled mightily under his new burden. He impatiently waited, deciding the old fisherman was walking far too slowly for his liking, when the fish suddenly tensed and started to flap back and forth. With his teeth clenched in surprise, Cathal tried to hold onto the slippery cod as it jumped from his arms.

Cathal watched in horror as the giant fish fell from his grasp, bounced off the side of the dock, and landed in the ocean. Gone. With a look of utter dismay, he watched after the dark shadow as it slipped deep under the lazy waves.

After a few moments, Cathal turned his head and could see the fisherman returning from the boat. The man had a confused look on his face.

As he approached, the fisherman asked, "Where is fish?"

Cathal just stood there, at a loss for words. A half mile to the north, a man was bleeding out, and here he was, trying to come up with a story on how a giant fish got away from him. He brought up his hand, closed his eyes, and pinched the bridge of his nose. *If the counsel of elders could see me now,* he thought. He opened his eyes and finally said, "I'm so sorry." His gaze then shifted to where the fish fell into the ocean.

"Fish is gone?"

Nodding his head glumly, Cathal said, "Fish is gone."

The old fisherman laughed, slapped Cathal on the shoulder and said, "You make worse fisherman than you do woodcutter, yes?"

Cathal cracked a smile, despite himself. "I'm so sorry," he repeated.

"Ah, you owe me a fish, then. Deal?" he said, as he pressed the fishing hook and line into Cathal's hands.

"Deal. I'll pay you back tomorrow, I promise." Cathal then turned around and ran back towards the logging camp.

As he ran past the logging camp, Cathal could see Domyan once again look up from the campfire, studying him with mild curiosity.

"You're wasting your time," growled the foreman, with an expressionless look on his face.

Cathal ignored him and hurried onward. A few moments later, he slowed to a jog as he saw the loggers gathered around the Turk. Several of the men had taken initiative and constructed a stretcher out of the branches from the birch trees.

Faolan looked up and said, "Did you get what you needed?"

Holding up the hook and line, Cathal nodded. He didn't say anything for a few moments, as he was still trying to catch his breath. Finally, as he stood beside the Turk with the broken leg, he said, "How is he holding up?"

"As well as could be expected, I suppose," said Faolan. He then gestured to a clump of birch bark that was soaking in a bucket of water. "Will that do?"

After a brief glance, Cathal nodded his head and said, "That will do. Thank you." He then looked at the hook and line in his hand. He would need to remove the barb from the hook before he could use it as a needle. "Does anyone have a hammer?"

The gathered Slavs and Turks looked at each other, shaking their heads.

With a heavy sigh, Cathal started to look on the ground for anything he could use. Finally, he saw a hand-sized rock and picked it up. He then knelt down and straightened out the hook with his fingers. With the rock in his right hand and the hook in his left, he held the hook against the ground and tapped at the barb with the rock. After a few minutes of pounding, the barb was mostly gone. It wasn't pretty, but it would have to do.

Cathal's skill as a doctor was evident, as he expertly worked on the man's open wound. Stitching the Turk's laceration took less than a half hour. He then took the soggy birch bark and carefully formed it around the man's broken leg.

"It will take a few hours for the cast to dry. We shouldn't move him until then."

The woodcutters looked at each other with concern. Finally, Faolan said, "It will be dark in a few hours and we're exposed out here, without proper weapons to defend ourselves. The wolves will approach at dusk. Staying here will put us all in danger."

Nodding his head, Cathal pursed his lips and thought for a moment, then said, "Okay. Let's put him on the stretcher. We'll take it slow."

Despite their slow progress, it only took a half hour to carry the Turk back to the campsite, where Domyan was impatiently waiting. The foreman stood up and walked over to the wounded Turk, examined his cast, then spat on the ground.

"I told you that you were wasting your time," he said, leering at Cathal. "Everyone who's survived a wolf attack out here, soon dies from the frothing disease. He'll be dead within a week." The foreman then walked around the gathering of loggers, looking each one in the eye. "For the last two hours, I haven't heard any trees falling. I haven't heard anyone working. I suppose you all think you're getting a full-day's pay for a half-day's work?" He stopped and leaned in towards one logger's face and screamed, "IS THAT WHAT YOU THINK?"

The man stepped back and stammered, "N-no foreman."

"What was that?" asked Domyan in a mocking tone, cupping his hand behind his ear.

"No foreman," the logger repeated.

"YOU'RE DAMN RIGHT!" Domyan yelled, with his spittle flying towards the man's face. He stepped back and pointed at the group. "You all want to work half a day? Then you get half-a-day's wage. Except for *you*." He moved his finger and pointed at Cathal. "You get nothing. Pull that shit again and you're fired."

Cathal clenched his jaw and kept his gaze focused on the ground before him. What else could he do? Something bothered him about Domyan: Earlier on, the foreman seemed pleased that Cathal was helping the injured Turk, but now Domyan was screaming at him for doing the same thing. It seemed like the foreman was teetering between emotional extremes, and under the present circumstances, that was a very dangerous thing, indeed.

Chapter 4

"Half-a-day's wages...my hairy Irish ass," spat Faolan. "We all worked an hour shy of a full day. This is an outrage."

Several of the Slavs around the campfire shot him a warning glance.

It was Mirko, the man with the red scar around his neck, who said, "Be careful what you say, Irishman. The foreman hears everything. But then again, what do I care?" He then reached for the bottle of mead that was passed around the campfire, and refilled his cup.

Cathal watched the man through the hazy smoke of the campfire. It was late at night, and the stars shown brightly overhead. Only a handful of men remained awake; the rest had retired for the evening. The Turkish man with the broken leg was reclining on an enormous log, softly snoring by the fire.

Closing his eyes, Cathal listened to the sound of burning firewood as it cracked and popped. He could hear snoring and the occasional slosh of mead, as the bottle was passed between workers. He stiffened as he heard the cabin door open behind him.

"Cathal. Get in here," barked the foreman.

With an apprehensive glance towards Faolan, Cathal rose to his feet and walked towards the cabin. What could the foreman possibly want at this hour? He slowly trudged over to the cabin, climbed the three steps of the rickety staircase and walked inside. The first thing he saw was an absolutely striking young woman in platinum blonde hair. She was sitting on a chair at the far end of the room. His heart skipped a beat as their eyes met. Was this Domyan's sister?

"Close the damn door," ordered Domyan.

Cathal reached out his hand and closed the door gently behind him. When he turned back around, he was momentarily startled when the foreman flicked a coin at him. He reflexively caught it with his other hand and looked at it – a silver coin!

"That's for today's work," said the foreman. He was leaning back in his chair with his bare feet propped up on his desk.

With more than a little trepidation, Cathal tried not to wince as he looked at the foreman's yellow, jagged toenails. "But I thought-"

"Never mind all that," interrupted Domyan. "Just keeping the workers on their toes, you understand. Don't tell the others. I don't want them to think that I've gone soft." He reached forward to grab a bottle of mead that was sitting on the desk. He then took a deep swig and let out a long sigh. Then, as if he'd just remembered something, he lifted his hand and gestured towards the young woman. "Have you met my sister, Danika?"

Nervously clasping his hands behind his back, Cathal said, "I have not. My name is-"

"I know who you are, Irishman," she said with a hint of amusement in her voice. "You're the doctor who has dreams of becoming a woodcutter."

Cathal was more than a bit annoyed at being cut off for the second time. In Ireland, he held a station of high repute. He offered her a curt nod and said, "I was simply trying to help." As he stood there uncomfortably, with his weight shifting from foot to foot, he tried to conceal his curiosity. The woman was absolutely stunning, with long blond hair framing her pale, angular face. Her eyelids and lips were tattooed black...such a strange look!

Danika leaned forward in her chair, canted her head and gave him a seductive grin, her black lips framing perfect white teeth. "You realize that you've just prolonged that poor man's suffering – instead of a quick death, he will now suffer excruciating pain and die slowly from the frothing disease."

"I'm sorry. I did not know." Despite himself, Cathal could not help but stare at the woman. It was obvious that she shared similar facial features to her brother, but the fact that Domyan's hair was black and her hair nearly white was such a strange contrast. He'd never seen that color of hair on a Slavic woman.

She snorted and gave him a bored look, twirling the end of a lock of her hair with the crook of her forefinger. "I imagine you're trying to figure out how I got my peculiar hair? My father was a handsome, blonde Swede. He happened to be the man who raped my mother while his war party was raiding our lands. Do you want to hear the amusing part? My mother still talks fondly of him, saying he was a much better lover than-"

"That's enough!" yelled Domyan, as he sat up and slammed his fist on the desk. "She said no such thing."

Danika pouted at her brother. She then stood up and walked slowly towards Cathal. She put her arms around his neck and looked into his eyes, enjoying his discomfort. Outside, a wolf's howl pierced the night sky. She looked over her shoulder and gazed out the window. "Oh, look. The moon's out." She then gave

Cathal a dazzling smile. "Do you know what that means?"

Taking a step back, Cathal narrowed his eyes and said, "Moon?"

At that moment, they could hear low growls and barks coming from outside. Urgent shouts from the loggers rang out, causing Domyan to jump to his feet. "Another attack!"

"W-What? What's happening?" stammered Cathal.

Domyan grabbed a pair of axes that were propped against the wall and threw one to Cathal. "Another damned wolf attack. Come on!" He marched over to the door and opened it, only to be greeted by two wolves staring at him with hateful eyes. As one of the wolves lunged at him, Domyan quickly slammed the door shut with a grunt. The door buckled from the impact of the wolf's charge, but held firm. He clenched his jaw and looked at his sister. He then reached for the door latch.

"No!" yelled Danika, lunging forward and putting her hands on his arm. "It's too late now. There's nothing we can do." She quickly ran to the cabin's only window and closed the wooden shutters. She then slid the latch shut, locking it tight.

The three stood helplessly as they listened to the commotion outside. Snarls and yelps from the wolves were drowned out by the anguished screams of the loggers. The grim sounds of battle continued, as what could only be the sound of dozens of wolves running through the logging camp, snapping and yipping at the unfortunate Slavs and Turks.

Domyan grabbed an old horn from the top of his desk and ran to the door. He set his foot a few inches in front of the door frame and steeled his nerves. With an apprehensive glance towards his sister, he brought the horn to his lips, opened the door a few inches and let out a loud blare, which rang out into the night.

Once again, a wolf charged the door, causing it to bend inward and nearly snap in protest. The animal's muzzle slipped through the crack of the door, snapping and growling as Domyan struggled to close it shut. "Help me!" he yelled.

Cathal charged forward and rammed the door with his shoulder, causing it to slam against the wolf's open snout. The animal yelped and pulled back, allowing them to close and lock the door.

Through labored breaths, Domyan said, "That should do it. The guardsmen in town should be here any minute."

Danika stood with her back against the wall, her eyes wide in dismay. "No. They'll all be slaughtered."

"There's no help for it now," said Domyan.

In the far distance, they could hear the braying of another horn.

"They've heard us!" said Domyan, a triumphant look on his face.

Just then, someone banged on the door, screaming to let him in. The three inside the cabin cast worried glances at each other, as they could hear the snarls of wolves outside, as well. Within seconds, the banging on the door stopped.

The chaos and clamor from the men outside continued on for several minutes. All the while, the blaring of horns could be heard, growing louder with each passing minute.

"This is nonsense. I *must* know what's going on!" said Domyan through clenched teeth.

"No!" shouted Danika.

The foreman would not be swayed. He grabbed the latch and carefully opened the door, just an inch, and peered through the crack. What he saw caused him to narrow his eyes and clench his jaw. There was a man-like *thing*, silhouetted by the tall flames of the campfire. The creature was hunched over, leering at him. Dozens of wolves were running about, and the ones that weren't running were feasting upon flayed and bloody carcasses.

At that moment, the guardsmen sounded their horns once again, as arrows started to whistle through the darkness. The creature in front of the campfire let out a hateful snarl, stooped down and tore off into the woods on all fours.

Domyan slammed the door shut and took a step backward.

A few moments later, all was quiet. "You can come out," said a voice from just outside the door.

"About damn time," mumbled Domyan, as he opened the battered front door.

Cathal stepped forward and his jaw went slack. What he saw was complete pandemonium. The lumber camp was a battlefield of twisted, bloody bodies. Over a dozen wolves lie dead around the perimeter of the campfire. Some of the wolves had arrows sticking out of their tough hides, while others had horrific gaping wounds from axes and swords.

A few terribly injured men were crawling on the ground, dragging their broken bodies towards the light of the campfire, begging for help. Garbled screams could be heard at the far end of the encampment.

"One of the worst attacks yet," spat the guardsman. "I lost at least two men."

Domyan gruffly stomped towards the campfire, snarling. He was clenching his fists while uttering Slavic curses. He counted three woodcutters dead, including the Turk who was recovering from his broken leg. Four woodcutters and two additional guardsmen were badly injured in the attack.

Cathal could see the völva making her rounds, tending to the Norsemen. She was carrying a large purse full of medical supplies, herbs and tinctures. The old woman made no effort to help the injured woodcutters.

Clenching his jaw, Cathal hurried over to the nearest logger – an aging Slavic man suffering from multiple bites on his legs and arms. He could dress and stitch the wounds, but it was hopeless. The injured men, woodcutters and guardsmen alike, were as good as dead.

In short order, the guardsmen collected their dead and dying and left the encampment without much fanfare, leaving Cathal to tend to the wounded Slavs and Turks. After he was done, Cathal turned to Domyan and said, "I'm surprised they came to help us. I thought the Norsemen wanted us all dead."

Domyan barked a short laugh and said, "The guardsmen don't give a damn about us. They would like nothing more than to see us slaughtered by the wolves, but they're under orders from the chieftain to keep the logging industry intact. If Birka loses its woodcutters, then the builders, all Norsemen mind you, won't have enough wood to build their longships and cabins."

The two men were startled when they heard a voice directly above them say, "I'm guessing it's safe to come down, now?"

Looking up, Cathal could see Faolan and two Slavic men sitting far above them in a large alder tree. "Did any of you get bit?" he asked.

As Faolan started to make his way down the tree, he said, "No. We climbed up here at the first sign of trouble."

"What happened to Biter?"

Faolan jumped to the ground and peered into the woods. He shook his head, cleared his throat and said, "I don't know. She killed one wolf and then this...*thing* started running towards the campfire. Biter backed away and tore off into the woods. I've never seen her frightened like that."

"What *thing*?" asked Cathal, furrowing his brow.

"Never mind all that," growled the foreman. "We have men to tend to and graves to dig.

Faolan gave a discrete warning glance to Cathal and mumbled, "I should go look for her."

"That wouldn't be wise, but I'm not going to stop you," said Domyan. He was standing by the campfire, staring into the flames. "Just be glad you're alive. What I saw a moment ago, standing right where I'm standing now...Well, where I come from, we have an old tale about a demon that has the head of a wolf and the legs of a horse. They have a voracious appetite, and eat human flesh."

"A psoglav," said Cathal.

A sinister grin crept across Domyan's face. "Ah, so you know of our traditions."

"Only a little."

Domyan turned around and stared at the Irishman. The flames of the campfire danced off his steely eyes as he said, "This place is cursed. Any fool can see that. It has been far too long since we showed the gods proper respect. They are punishing us for our transgressions. It is time we made an offering to Veles." He then walked towards the cabin. Before opening the door, he turned around and said, "Get your shovels and start digging. I want those graves ready by sunrise."

After the foreman slammed the door shut, Faolan turned to Cathal and asked, "Veles? Who the hell is Veles?"

A rueful smile crossed Cathal's lips. "Who the hell, indeed. Veles is the Slavic god of the underworld. He shares similarities to the Christian's concept of Satan. Tell me, Faolan, are you a Christian?"

"Like all good Irishmen, yes. And you?"

Shaking his head, Cathal said, "I am not what people would call a good Irishman."

"Then what do you believe?"

Cathal canted his head down and pursed his lips. "That is a conversation for another day. Come on, let's get those shovels." As they walked towards the tool shed, he asked, "Does Domyan expect us to dig graves all night, then work a full day tomorrow?"

With raised eyebrows, Faolan said, "What do you think?"

"Unbelievable," whispered Cathal. He reached his hand to the pouch tied to his belt and felt the outline of a silver coin. Would he receive extra money for digging the graves? He doubted it. It was almost comical – a silver coin a day to risk one's life.

They found a suitable clearing to the west of the logging camp and began to dig. The ground was hard and full of stones, slowing their progress. They planted several torches in the ground, which provided a flickering light that held the dark night at bay.

Casting a worried glance into the forest surrounding them, Faolan said, "Did you notice that none of the Slavic woodcutters are helping us dig graves? This is beyond dangerous – those wolves could come back at any time."

Cathal just shook his head and said, "Let it go. I've traveled around the world, and every nationality on this earth looks after their own. The Slavs are no different."

Letting out a series of curses, punctuated by thrusting his shovel into the hard dirt, Faolan asked, "What do you think Domyan is going to do? He mentioned an offering."

Stopping for a moment to rub his raw hands, Cathal said, "I'm not sure of the ritual he has in mind, but I do know a few things about Veles."

"Such as?"

Cathal exhaled sharply and began digging once again. "Have you heard of the Norse gods Thor and Loki?"

"Of course."

"Well, the Norse people have a myth about a god of thunder who does battle with a giant serpent. The Slavs have a similar myth – *their* god of thunder battles a dragon. For the Norse, Thor is the god of thunder. The Slavic god of thunder is Perun, and he is much older. Perun is the eternal enemy of Veles, god of the underworld. But Veles is a god of many things: the underworld, the earth, the water, and the forest."

Faolan looked at him sharply and said, "The forest..."

"Yes. That's why I think Domyan is going to make an offering to Veles – to appease the spiteful god and bring calm to the forest."

"Do you really think that is the reason?"

"I do. It was not difficult to draw conclusions. Every Slav knows that Veles punishes oath-breakers with torment and disease. The wolves have infected the workers with the frothing disease. Domyan must think the frothing disease is a curse from the gods, and when he made no attempt to appease Veles, the angry god sent wolves to attack them. It makes sense, in an odd sort of way.

"Sounds like a bunch of superstitious nonsense to me," snorted Faolan.

"Maybe so, maybe so," said Cathal. He was exhausted from working all day. The prospect of working through the night and the entire next day ebbed at his mind. *Stay strong*, he told himself. He brought his hand up to his face and rubbed his bloodshot eyes. As he opened his eyes and looked up, he could see something moving in the treeline. The shadow then accelerated, and seemed to run towards them. Something big. His legs froze as he pointed towards the approaching creature. He then started to stammer; so frightened that he couldn't form words.

Faolan jerked his head up and squinted his eyes. The creature was just beyond the torchlight, closing in fast. He held his shovel defensively before him, his knuckles white. He let out a short gasp through clenched teeth and urgently whispered, "No, no, no..."

The creature, with its head low to the ground, loped into view and ran towards the two men with wild abandon. Its jaws were open and its tongue was hanging out of its mouth. It had an exuberant expression was on its face. Faolan relaxed his grip on his shovel as his eyes widened in disbelief...It was Biter!

The wolfhound ran at Faolan and barreled paws first into him. So happy was the creature, that it bounded around the Irishman and let out a series of excited yelps.

Faolan laughed, tripped backward and fell to the ground, only to be smothered by the slobbering licks of the wolfhound. "Biter, stop it!"

A look of concern crossed Cathal's eyes. He grabbed one of the torches from the ground and held it over the dog, examining the wolfhound's coat for any sign of bleeding or damage.

Faolan immediately understood what Cathal was doing. He sat up and asked, "Do you see anything?"

After a moment, Cathal let out a heavy sigh of relief and said, "No, I don't see any blood. I think she's safe."

"Thank god."

"You shouldn't thank your Christian god," said a familiar voice. "It was not He who saved your dog, but Veles." Domyan walked towards the two men with a smug look on his face. He stood before the torchlight, his shadow looming over the shallow grave. "Stop your digging and come back to camp. I have prayed to the gods and they have given me guidance." Without further explanation, the foreman turned and walked back into the woods.

With a puzzled look, Faolan tilted his head towards Cathal and whispered, "What do you think he meant by that?"

Cathal shook his head as he watched the foreman walk into the darkness of night. He then let out a long exhale and said, "Nothing good."

Chapter 5

As Cathal and Faolan approached the logging camp, they saw Domyan, Danika, and the remaining woodcutters gathered next to the dead and dying. Cathal made a mental note: three of the woodcutters, including the previously injured Turk, were dead and lying on stretchers. Four additional workers were badly injured, leaving a workforce of only five remaining loggers, not including the foreman and his sister.

"Ah, everyone's here," said the foreman. Domyan was carrying a bow and had a quiver of arrows slung over his shoulder. Cathal reasoned the bow must be for protection. "The ritual site is at the eastern shore, about a half mile from here. Let's move out!"

Crinkling his brow, Cathal watched as the workers dragged the stretchers of dead men off to the east. *Ritual site?* What did Domyan have in mind? He then looked at the four injured men – those unfortunate souls who would be dead from the frothing disease within a week. They were all staggering drunk, barely able to walk unassisted. *What was going on?* He was besieged with too many questions; questions only the foreman could answer.

It was a slow trek towards the shore. Cathal looked up at the night sky. The distant stars glimmered through the tree branches overhead.

They were traveling single file down a narrow dirt path. Domyan and his sister led the way. They were carrying torches that barely cut through the darkness. Three of the woodcutters were dragging dead men on stretchers, while two of the loggers were helping the injured walk.

Not a word was spoken as they trudged down the ominous forest path, until one of the Turkish men, the only remaining Turk that wasn't dead or injured, started to mumble and curse under his breath.

"Quiet!" said Domyan, as he turned and gave the woodcutter a withering stare.

The Turkish man glowered at the foreman, but kept his mouth shut.

Despite their slow progress, it did not take long for the small group to make it to the eastern shore. Cathal gazed at the moonlit waves, as they lazily lapped against the rocky shore. The men who were dragging the dead set their stretchers down and rubbed their hands. They gazed upward and apprehensively looked at a giant tree that had ropes slung over its thick branches.

Cathal counted seven ropes. It did not take long to deduce that each rope was fated for a dead or dying woodcutter. He was jolted out of his contemplations when the Turkish man started yelling at Domyan in his native tongue, pointing his finger at the giant oak. The foreman simply stood there, implacable.

Finally, the Turk spat at Domyan's feet and yelled in broken Norse, "I quit! Finished!" He then stomped off down the trail with his hands clenched into fists.

"Coward!" yelled Domyan after the retreating man. "I just lost half my workforce, and another worker just runs off? That's the last time I hire a Turk, you motherless dog!" In a rage, he reached for an arrow in his quiver, but thought better of it.

The Turk didn't bother with a response. He simply continued to walk down the narrow trail, soon lost to the darkness.

Ignoring the deserter, Domyan ordered his men to drag the dead workers to the tree and slip the nooses over their heads. The four injured woodcutters were so inebriated, they barely understood what was happening.

Faolan nudged Cathal, leaned in and whispered, "Aren't you going to do something?"

"What would you have me do?" Cathal whispered back. "There's over a half-dozen superstitious men who think this ritual sacrifice will solve their problems. Do you want me to tell them otherwise? What good could *that* possibly do? Besides, the men who were bitten are going to die anyway. If this sacrifice gives the other men peace of mind, who am I to argue?"

With more than a little apprehension, Faolan shook his head and said, "I may not be the most saintly of Christians, but this is an affront to god. It's an abomination!"

Cathal shot him a warning glance. "Not another word, if you know what's good for you," he said in a hushed tone. From the corner of his eye, he could see the foreman staring at him.

Domyan broke off his withering gaze and approached his workers, pointing at the tree. In his native Slavic tongue, he instructed his remaining loggers to start pulling on the ropes, hoisting the injured and dead aloft.

One of the injured men, less inebriated than the others, started to panic as he was hoisted into the air. He lurched to and fro, trying to shake himself free.

Without a moment's hesitation, Domyan grabbed an arrow from his quiver and notched it in his bow. He mumbled, "Coward," as he pulled back then released the drawstring.

The arrow pierced the man's lower stomach, causing him to stiffen, then slump. He then started to wretch and sob uncontrollably as Domyan marched towards him, muttering under his breath. The foreman grabbed the injured man by the tunic and started to punch him in the face with savage ferocity, causing the man to lose consciousness after the third blow.

Domyan was incensed. He had a wild, almost rapturous gleam in his eye. As the remaining victims were being hoisted upward, Domyan raised his bow to the night sky and shouted, "Veles has cursed this entire island – an island owned by the Northlanders. The *true* gods are angry at the Norsemen's false religion. The Vikings take what they want – they rape and pillage and we do nothing to stop them. Tonight we show the true gods that we are ready to take back what is rightfully ours. We will not sit back and accept the meager scraps the Northlanders throw at us. As we make this sacrifice to Veles, he will curse our enemies and strengthen our resolve!"

He then gestured for his workers to tie down the ropes. With a brief glance towards one another, the loggers tied the ropes to the lower branches of the oak tree, causing the bodies of the unfortunate victims to twist in the wind.

"Veles, this is our gift to you," shouted Domyan. "Take these men as a token of our faith, and bless us with the power to overcome the hated Norsemen."

Cathal averted his eyes, as the sacrificial victims twisted and twitched in the air high above him. It wasn't the manner of death that troubled him, but the deity to whom the men were being sacrificed. Veles, dark god of the underworld, steeped in magic and trickery. Veles, ruler of the dead. Veles, the god who could shape-shift into any man or beast.

While Domyan sang liturgies to his blasphemous god, the small gathering of Slavic men hummed along. They were transfixed by the ritual, looking up with fervent devotion at the sacrificial victims swinging overhead.

All except one.

Mirko averted his eyes and started to grumble under his breath, deeply troubled. As the loggers chanted and sang, the man with the scarred throat marched off into the woods, towards camp.

"Ah, Mirko, come back!" yelled Domyan. "I thought *you* of all people would appreciate a good hanging!" The foreman laughed and raised his hands towards the night sky. For the next few minutes, he congratulated the hanged men for their bravery, assuring them they would soon meet Veles.

The hanged men twitched and jerked in response.

Cathal was troubled. As all eyes were transfixed upon the men slowly dying above them, *his* eyes were scanning the forest. It took him a moment to see it, but when he did, it was as if the world had dropped out from under him. Dozens of wolves formed a half circle around them, just beyond the light of the torches. The torchlight barely reflecting off their amber eyes. There was one set of eyes that was several feet higher than the rest, staring directly at him.

He stumbled backward and fell over an old tree stump. So enraptured were the Slavs, that no one noticed him, save for one – Danika was laughing at him, an enraptured countenance glazed in her visage.

Domyan then turned and noticed Cathal. He had an amused expression etched on his scarred face. With a slow, almost languid movement, the foreman took an arrow from his quiver, notched his bow and pointed it straight at him. He pointed the arrow at Cathal's heart for a few moments, enjoying the apprehension in the Irishman's eyes. Then, with a smirk, he turned and aimed the arrow at one of the hanged men and released the drawstring. The arrow whistled through the air and punctured the victim's chest. The unfortunate man gasped and gurgled, his eyes rolling back in his head.

The foreman continued to shoot arrows into the sacrificial victims until they finally stopped twitching. All that could be heard was the creak of ropes against sturdy tree branches. Cathal simply sat there on the ground, holding his head in his hands. A light touch on his shoulder caused him to look upward. It was Danika.

She bent over and whispered, "Get up. He despises weakness."

Weakness? He almost let out a spiteful laugh as he climbed to his feet. He was not lamenting the grisly manner of death – he'd seen far worse on the battlefields across Frankia and Ireland. No, he was lamenting the dark ritual. He knew the power of the dark Slavic gods; he knew they were treacherous. Veles would answer the call, of that he had no doubt. But he also knew that Veles took away more than he bestowed, no matter the sacrifice.

Cathal looked to the treeline once again. The wolves were gone. He could see the faint glow of twilight from the horizon, as the sun dared to shed light on the blasphemies of man.

"It is done," said Domyan. He then turned and addressed his workers. "Go back to camp and get a few hours rest. We still have a full day's work ahead of us."

Domyan led the way, with his men following in single file behind him. They walked in silence. As the morning light washed over the land, birds started to sing and chirp, giving a stark contrast to the night's horrific events.

The woodcutters entered the logging camp and trudged to their sleeping quarters without a word, ignoring the blood-stained ground. Cathal stumbled up the steps to the worker's cabin, exhausted from the chaotic events of the day. He fell upon his cot and stared at the crossbeams on the ceiling. Exhausted as he was, it took him nearly a full hour to fall asleep, as he contemplated the treachery of dark gods and deranged foremen.

* * * * * * *

In his dream, he was walking down a twisted path through the dark wood of the forest. Looming shadows surrounded him, shifting and stretching. Overhead, the sun quickly arced over the sky, then descended and gave way to the moon. A minute later, night passed into day. The cycle of day and night quickly repeated – every minute, another day, another night. During each cycle of night, the moon became fatter, more ominous.

Finally, the full moon shown directly overhead and stopped. The moon-struck shadows froze in place as hundreds of hungry, amber eyes peered at him from a faraway field.

In a panic, Cathal stepped off the path and ran towards a light that was shining just beyond the horizon. As he ran, shadows from the trees contorted around him. They were clutching at his limbs and slowing his progress. The harder he pushed forward, the stronger the shadows became. The shadows were like quicksand, pulling him back from the light. Despite it all, he continued onward, towards the light.

And then he saw it – a raging inferno, reaching up to the heavens. Inside the inferno were dozens of screaming men, reaching out to him; pleading for mercy. He stood before the inferno, feeling the heat blast his skin, listening to the cries of damned men.

A hand softly touched his shoulder. With trepidation, he turned around and looked up. It was the psoglav – that Slavic demon with the head of a wolf and legs of a horse. It towered over him, smelling of rotted, diseased flesh. The creature curled back its lips, revealing jagged iron teeth. It then spoke in an spectral voice, "One of us-"

* * * * * *

"Get up," grumbled the foreman, as he roughly kicked the cot.

Cathal opened his eyes to see Domyan glowering over him. He glanced at the other cots. The loggers were sitting up, rubbing the sleep from their eyes. How long had they been asleep? Not long, judging by the morning light washing into the rickety cabin.

"Get dressed and meet me outside," said Domyan. "We're going into town to get more workers. Hurry up." The foreman then turned around and marched outside.

Cathal sat there for a moment, rubbing his temples.

"Get going," said a raspy voice. It was Mirko. "When the foreman says hurry up, you hurry up!"

Nodding his head, Cathal slowly stood up and stretched his lower back. He was too tired to argue. He put on his clothes, noticing the stares from the Slavic men in the cabin. Why did Domyan choose *him* to go to town? He then looked down at his hands. They were still blistered and raw.

"Get going, Irishman," repeated Mirko.

"Yeah," sniffed Cathal, clearing his throat. As he walked outside, he squinted his eyes against the morning sun. Judging by its position in the sky, he only had a couple hours of sleep.

"What a night, eh?" said Domyan. He seemed to be in unusually good spirits, despite what had just transpired. Motioning for Cathal to follow him, the foreman continued, "In the last few months, I've lost a total of five woodcutters. I complained to the chieftain, of course. He just brushed it off, barely compensating me for my losses. The chieftain never said as much, but it was obvious that since the workers weren't of Norse descent, they were expendable. But last night – seven more dead! That brings the total to a dozen dead men. Not even the chieftain can ignore that."

"Is it the chieftain's responsibility to supply you with workers?" asked Cathal.

Domyan shot him a caustic glance. "It's the chieftain's responsibility to make sure the woodcutters have safe working conditions. When he doesn't live up to that responsibility, he must compensate me, either by coin or by replacement workers."

Cathal considered the foreman's words. It seemed strange to him that the Norsemen would allow foreigners to take over certain industries in Birka. But the economics and politics of this town were beyond his concerns. He was here for an entirely different reason. Besides, there were more pressing matters at hand. He turned to the foreman and said, "There seems to be something other than wolves in these woods."

The foreman grunted and said, "So it seems."

"Any ideas on what that might be?"

With an arched eyebrow, Domyan replied, "I have more than a few ideas on what that thing might be. The Slavic workers say it's a psoglav, a wolf-headed creature steeped in Germanic lore. But if you talk with the Turks, they say the creature is an erbörü, a monster that is half man, half wolf. Of course, the Norsemen have their own tales of werewolves. Interesting, is it not? Three distinct cultures in different parts of the world that have similar myths. Tell me, Irishman. Do your people also have legends of werewolves?

Cathal nodded his head. "Over five-hundred years ago, there was a Christian bishop by the name of Saint Patrick. He tried to convert the people of Ireland to Christianity. Some of those people held onto their old beliefs, so Saint Patrick put a curse upon them, turning them into werewolves. There's also an Irish legend of a mercenary group who could change into wolves. They did not fight for money, but for the flesh of newborn children. Even so, it was a price the kings of Ireland willingly paid to repel invaders."

Domyan remained silent for a time, considering Cathal's words. Finally, he said, "Do you see? There is a connection between wolf and man, no matter the culture."

"The chronicle of werewolves goes back even further than you might imagine," continued Cathal. "Even Greek and Roman historians have mentioned it in their texts. The first instance I discovered was from over two-thousand years ago, when King Lycaon of Arcadia killed his own son and offered the remains to Zeus. Zeus was so outraged, he transformed King Lycaon into a wolf."

"Zeus?"

"He's the most powerful of the Greek gods."

The foreman started to laugh. "Ha! You're a doctor, a historian, *and* a fine woodcutter!" He then grew more serious. "You seem to know a lot about history, for a doctor."

"I can read and write in Latin. It's simply a hobby of mine."

"Latin, eh?" Domyan grumbled. "I never had use for the written word. Bunch of nonsense."

Cathal remained silent. His conversations with brutish men usually devolved in such fashion. No matter. They were now walking through the northern part of Birka, towards the chieftain's longhouse. All manner of people – Norse, Slavs, Turks, Franks and English, bustled among the dusty dirt road. He could see shops and markets selling all types of goods. Some of the booths offered smoked meats and fish, while others offered jewelry and trinkets. He made a mental note of one booth that sold herbs and tinctures.

"The chieftain's longhouse is up ahead," said Domyan. "Stay quiet and do what I tell you. The chieftain is the stingiest man I have ever met. If we're to get new workers, we need to impress upon him how dire our situation is."

Cathal crinkled his brow. What was the foreman up to? He still didn't know why the foreman selected *him* for this little expedition. As they approached the longhouse, he could see a guardsman standing in front of the door.

"What is your business?" asked the guardsman, his bored eyes casually sizing up the foreman.

"What do you think?" barked Domyan, pointing his finger in the guard's face. "Tell the chieftain I need a word with him."

The guardsman sneered contemptuously, then cracked open the door and yelled inside, "Torsten, the foreman of the logging camp wants a word."

After a moment, a voice from inside the longhouse said, "Why am I not surprised? Send him in."

Swinging the door wide open, the guardsman jerked his head to the side, motioning for them to enter. Once they were inside, the guard slammed the door shut behind them.

Cathal was surprised to find the chieftain sitting at a table, playing a board game with a little girl. His daughter, perhaps?

"Give me a moment," said Torsten, his eyes intently studying the board. "You wouldn't know it to look at her, but young Ulla here is the best Hnefatafl player in Birka! Have you ever played?"

"I'm afraid not," said Domyan with thinly-veiled indifference.

Torsten kept his eyes on the game. "It's rather simple, once you understand the rules. The board is an eleven-by-eleven grid. One player attacks with white stones, while the other player defends with his black stones. The defending player must protect his king by moving it to a corner grid, or lose the game."

"I don't have time for such things," replied Domyan in a listless tone.

"Ha! And yet you have time to come here and bother me with your nonsense. I swear, if you want workers, go out and find them! How is this my problem?"

"It's *your* problem because the only workers available right now are Norsemen, and they refuse to work for me!"

"Rightly so. It's dangerous in those woods," snorted Torsten.

The young girl laughed and clapped her hands.

Domyan gave the girl a deadpan stare, then continued, "Look at this man's hands." He gestured for Cathal to hold up his hands. "All of my woodcutters are working their fingers to the bone just to fill orders for *your* longboats. Now that half of my workforce is gone, we won't be able to fill those orders."

Ah, so *that's* why the foreman brought me along, thought Cathal.

With an exasperated sigh, Torsten pushed away from the table and stood up. He was a tall, barrel-chested man with long red hair and a braided beard. He marched towards Domyan and stood before him, crossing his arms on his chest and tilting his head to the side. His gray eyes had a slightly menacing bearing.

The foreman stood his ground and offered the chieftain a half-smirk. Domyan was nearly as tall as the chieftain, but his body was starkly different. He was lean, almost gaunt, with muscular shoulders and a cruel, scar-ridden face framed by straight black, shoulder-length hair.

After a tense moment, Torsten finally said, "I suppose I could spare a few slaves. It will cost you two silver a day, per slave."

"Two silver? For a slave? I pay my workers *one* silver a day. How am I expected to turn a profit? I'll give you one silver a day per worker, and you'll take the deal, if you want enough lumber for your longships and cabins."

Torsten stood there and scratched his beard. He started to grumble under his breath, then a glint came to his eye and a mischievous smile spread across his face. "Alright, then. I suppose I can spare three workers for that price. You'll find them in the slave's quarters. Their names are Greger, Gottfrid, and Gustav. The guardsman at the front door will show you the way. Anything else?"

Raising one eyebrow, Domyan said, "Only three workers? I lost seven last night."

"Seven? The guardsmen told me you lost three."

"Three workers were killed, and four more were badly injured. You know they're as good as dead. The frothing disease will take them soon enough."

Cathal shot a glance at the foreman. Domyan didn't mention the ritual by the shore last night. Interesting. He sighed inwardly and looked at his blistered hands.

"Well, three is all I can spare. Be grateful I'm giving you any workers at all. This meeting is finished!" The chieftain turned and walked back to the table where his daughter was patiently waiting.

"Your turn!" said the young girl.

Domyan scowled and stomped out the door, with Cathal following close behind him. Once outside, the foreman exchanged a few words with the guardsman, then turned to Cathal and said, "I need to round up the slaves and conclude some other matters here. Go back to camp and start working." He then turned and followed the guardsman to the slave quarters.

Cathal watched as the two men marched off. He then turned and walked towards the market. He needed some supplies, and there was also the matter of repaying the old fisherman for the cod he lost at the docks yesterday.

Was that only yesterday? He let out a heavy sigh. Seven men had died since then. Nine, including the two guardsmen. He was witness to a brutal ritual, and he learned that his foreman was fervently devoted to one of the dark Slavic gods. There was a strong likelihood that the wolves would attack again, and something unexplained was walking amongst those frightful creatures.

Yet he continued to stay. He shook his head in exasperation. He would need to send word back to the council. Matters in Birka were far more dire than the elders had suspected.

Chapter 6

Strong winds blew dust and debris down the busy dirt road. Cathal stood before one of the booths that lined the market and perused the selection of herbs and tinctures. An old Norse woman working behind the booth kept a sharp eye on him; it was clear she didn't trust foreigners.

Cathal was pleased to find myrrh and comfrey leaves, as well as a variety of other herbs for sale. None of the herbs were labeled, but he was able to identify most of the dried extracts. His eyes then fell upon the herb he was searching for. He pointed at the small jar and asked, "Wolfsbane?"

The old woman nodded and said, "Hunting wolves, are we?"

"Yes. Something like that," he replied with a grim smile. Wolfsbane was used to coat arrowheads and animal traps to poison wolves and bears. Even whalers used the poison to tip their spears.

He pointed to the myrrh, comfrey, calendula and wolfsbane, and the woman put a portion of each herb into separate small pouches. After paying the woman, he sauntered over to a booth that was selling fish and other meats. He was pleased to see a cod even larger than the one he'd lost yesterday.

Luckily, he had just enough money to purchase the fish. He held the giant cod in both hands and walked towards the docks. The slimy fish burned the broken blisters on his hands. At least he wasn't in danger of it jumping into the ocean, he mused. Cathal squinted as the howling wind blew dust and dirt into his eyes. He then let out a sigh; he didn't see the old fisherman anywhere.

Cathal realized that after two meetings with the man, he still didn't know the old fisherman's name. He finally found a dockworker who recognized his description. The man pointed towards the tavern.

"He's at lunch," said the tall Norseman, as he lumbered past.

Cathal let out a long exhale and trudged back towards town. A few minutes later, he found himself in the tavern, looking over the smoky din of laborers and fishermen. He soon found a familiar face hunched over a tall cup of mead. He walked towards the fisherman and threw the giant fish down on the table with a smug look on his face.

The old fisherman leaned forward with surprise and said, "Ah, that's a good one!"

"Glad you like it. The man who sold it to me said it was the finest cod in the ocean."

"Ha! To the merchants in town, *every* fish is the finest in the ocean!" He motioned for Cathal to take a seat.

As he pulled up a chair and sat down, Cathal said, "I must apologize. This is the third time we've met, and I still don't know your name."

"Mats. My friends call me Old Mats." He grabbed the smoking pipe that was cinched in his belt and lit it with the candle that was sitting on the table. The candle fluttered and sputtered as he drew air. He then blew out a large plume of gray smoke.

"My name is Cathal." He watched as the smoke slowly dissipated into the air. "I must say, I don't see too many Norsemen smoking."

With a half-smile, Mats nodded. He thoughtfully puffed on his pipe and said, "It's a habit I picked up from the Turks. I taught them how to play dice, and they taught me how to smoke." The old man then leaded in with a grave look on his face. "That was some nasty business up in the woods last night."

"You heard about that?"

"Of course! A death in one of the camps always gets the tongues wagging, but five dead in one night? It's unheard of! By far the worst attack yet." He then shook his head and looked down his nose at his pipe. "Nasty, nasty business."

"The Slavs think the Norsemen are behind the attacks," said Cathal. "They say the wolves only attack the foreigners."

Old Mat's eyes widened in surprise. "What now? That simply isn't true! The chieftain lost two guardsmen last night protecting the woodcutters."

"Yes, but the way the Slavs tell it, the guardsmen *had* to intervene. Otherwise there would be a rebellion in the camps. Industry comes first, welfare of the migrants come second, they say."

With a snort, Old Mats shook his head. "Nonsense. Those men in the camps are encroaching on the wolves' territory. The Norsemen could see what was happening, and so they got jobs working close to Birka, leaving the more dangerous jobs for the foreigners. The only thing the Norsemen are guilty of is taking care of their own; giving preferable jobs to their own kinsmen."

Cathal paused for a moment, scratching his short-cropped beard. "That's what I figured. There's something odd going on in that logging camp, and I can't quite put my finger on it."

"How so?"

The Irishman crinkled his brow and considered for a moment. Finally, he said, "The foreman and his sister are two of the strangest people I've ever met. If I didn't see the creature while in their company, I'd swear one of them was the werewolf."

Old Mats straightened in his chair and gave him a puzzled look. "Werewolf?"

Cathal leaned in and said in a hushed tone, "There's something in those woods other than the wolves. It's something that walks *amongst* the wolves, upright – on two legs!"

The fisherman's puzzled look turned to one of concern. He took the pipe out of his mouth and said, "Men who suffer through horrific experiences sometimes see things that aren't there. Their minds play tricks on them, trying to make sense of what happened. It's nothing to be ashamed of."

Leaning back in his chair, Cathal let out a long sigh and said, "Perhaps." He then looked around the pub and asked, "Are there any barmaids around here?"

"They're about, but they're slower to attend the migrants."

"Figures...I need to get back to work, anyway," lamented Cathal. He then added, "Do you know who I could ask to deliver a message to Ireland?"

"I supposed I could forward your message to the right people."

Nodding his head, Cathal took a folded piece of parchment out of one of his pouches and handed it to the fisherman. "I appreciate it. There's a Viking presence in Dublin, and longboats regularly come from abroad to trade with the city. Make sure this message gets to the Abbot of Finglas Monastery in Dublin. It's very important. The fate of Birka may depend on it."

"The fate of Birka?" The old fisherman looked dubious. "Surely it's a tragedy that all those men died last night, but Birka has over five-hundred residents, most of them hardened men. I think we'll be just fine."

Cathal pushed away from the table and stood up. "Just between you and me – *nine* people died last night. The foreman of the lumber camp had the injured men put to death. There are circumstances occurring here that are far graver than mere wolf attacks. Make sure that note gets into the right hands."

As Cathal approached the lumber camp, he scowled and lamented his luck. He doubted the note would reach the monastery in time. It would take weeks for the message to reach Dublin. And then what? He had a nagging suspicion that whatever transpired here on Birka, would be long over before the abbot of Finglas Monastery could do anything about it.

He stopped by the campfire, knelt down, and untied the pouches of herbs from his belt. He then grabbed a jug of water and poured it into a pan, took out a few pinches of the various herbs he just purchased, and mixed it into the water. He kept a careful eye on the measurements. After the mixture had dissolved enough, he placed a few rags into the liquid, letting it soak thoroughly. He then squeezed the excess water out of the rags and put the pan away. The herbs now infused the rags; they would act as a disinfectant and healing agent.

Cathal could hear the sound of chopping wood far in the distance. With an agitated exhale, he wrapped his hands with the rags and grabbed an ax from the tool shed. If Domyan found him dawdling around the campfire while the others were working, he'd never hear the end of it. He slowly walked to the northern edge of the lumber camp with the ax slung over his shoulder. He was exhausted. Judging by the position of the sun, he had another four hours until the end of the workday.

He wondered how the other men were holding up. The survivors had just escaped a brutal wolf attack. They saw their fellow workers being ripped apart. The Slavs seemed like hardened men, but that type of traumatic event would affect anyone. How much further could they be pushed until they reached their breaking point? Not long, Cathal surmised, if the wolf attacks continued.

But where else could the workers go? Most of the loggers were Slavs – they couldn't find jobs anywhere else. It 's the only reason Domyan could get away with paying them so little.

Cathal shook his head in disgust. The upper class always took advantage of the lower class; it was the way of the world. It didn't even matter that the workers were of the same nationality – the elite of Norse and Irish societies exploited their own workers in the same way.

When he finally reached his work area at the north end of camp, Cathal tightened the bindings on his hands and hefted his ax. He winced as he gripped his hands around the haft of the weapon. With the first few swings of the ax, the blisters on his hands reopened. He cursed under his breath; it was going to be a long afternoon.

Heavily perspiring under the summer sun, Cathal stopped and set his ax against the old birch tree. The rags on his hands were thoroughly soaked with blood. As he peeled back the fabric from his skin, he clenched his jaw and drew air between his teeth. Pain pulsed in his hands with each heartbeat, as blood freely streamed down his forearms and onto the ground.

"Ready to call it a day?" asked a voice behind him. It was Faolan.

Cathal turned around and waved. "Just a moment." As he knelt down to grab the bloody rags off the ground, Biter loped up and started to lick his hands. He laughed and winced at the same time; the dog's rough tongue tugged at his blisters and raw skin.

"Better watch it. They don't call her Biter for nothing," laughed Faolan.

"Ah, maybe you're right. What good is a woodcutter with no hands?" said Cathal. Grabbing his ax, he fell in step with Faolan as they walked back to camp. "Have you seen the new workers?"

"Me? No. It's just been me and Biter working alone. Why, have *you* seen them?"

Cathal shook his head. "Not yet. All I know, is that Domyan spoke to the chieftain this morning and acquired three Norse slaves. Brothers, from what I hear."

"Well, we could sure use the help. I hope they're hard workers. Domyan doesn't put up with slackers."

With a snort, Cathal said, "So I hear."

As the two men entered the clearing of the logging camp, they could see most of the woodcutters sitting around the campfire. Three men with blond hair were also sitting by the fire, with their backs facing them. The Norse slaves, perhaps?

Domyan was standing in the middle of the gathering. He was madly waving his arms and pointing at the three blond men. *What was going on?* As Cathal walked within hearing range, he was puzzled as to why the foreman was shouting obscenities at the slaves.

"Does the chieftain think I'm some kind of idiot?" shouted Domyan. "I have quotas to fill, and he gives me the oldest, most decrepit workers on the island. This is outrageous!"

"We can work just as hard as any of you," said one of the slaves.

"Don't kid yourself, brother. A Norseman can work *twice* as hard as any foreigner," said another slave.

Cathal and Faolan walked around the perimeter of the campfire to get a look at the new arrivals. What they saw was almost comical – the three Norse brothers were ancient; they were well into their seventies. They didn't have blond hair, but grayish-white hair. One of the old men seemed to shake and quiver, for no reason at all.

Domyan brought his fingers to the bridge of his nose and closed his eyes. "I swear to the gods, if you senile old fools don't pull your weight tomorrow, I'm going to put a whip to you."

"You'll be putting the whip to your other workers, when you see that we chop twice as much wood as they do!" said one of the slaves.

The foreman slowly opened his eyes and said, "You know what bothers me about you Vikings? You borrow everything from other cultures and call it your own. Even your weak gods are mere imitations of the true Slavic gods."

"If our gods are so weak, then why is it that the Slavs work for us, and not the other way around? Are Norsemen *not* the dominant power in this world? That is a true measure of the power of the gods – the gods simply reflect the strength of their people!"

"Your gods are ridiculous," laughed Domyan. "Why, you even have a squirrel god. What was his name? Ratatat-something?"

"Ratatoskr," said one of the slaves, while chewing on his gums.

"Yes! Ratatoskr, the mighty god of acorns! Veles flees in terror from the god of tree-rats!" Domyan threw his head back and laughed, as did most of the loggers around the campfire.

The old slave looked dejected. "At least we have a sense of humor about things."

Domyan grew serious and spoke in a low, measured tone. "Yes...sense of humor. You Norsemen seem to think *everything* is amusing, don't you? You think foreigners being torn apart by wolves is amusing, and you think the way you exploit migrants is simply delightful."

"You would speak to a slave of exploitation? I've lived my entire life as a slave, and you don't hear me complaining about it. That's the problem with you foreigners. You think we owe you something, and then you're bitter because we just don't give you what you want on a silver platter."

Cathal could see the foreman's eye start to twitch.

With a clenched jaw, Domyan shifted his leg back and kicked a flaming log from the campfire towards the startled slave. The log arced through the air, narrowly missing the Norseman's head.

"I hope your back is as strong as your words," said Domyan, as he stomped off to his cabin and slammed the door shut behind him.

The woodcutters exchanged worried glances. They had never seen anyone stand up to the foreman before; certainly not some decrepit old slaves! A few quiet moments passed. All that could be heard was the crackle and snap of the campfire.

Worried that Domyan might storm back out of his cabin, the loggers stood up and walked back to their living quarters. As they strolled past the campfire, one of the woodcutters stopped and pointed his finger at one of the slaves. "Watch yourselves," said Mirko in his raspy voice. "I've seen the foreman beat a man to death for less."

Chapter 7

The next morning the loggers were awoken in the usual manner – with Domyan kicking on the door and yelling various insults about their laziness and ineptitude.

After the foreman stopped kicking the door, the loggers groaned and rolled out of their cots. Most of the workers were uttering curses in Slavic, a few were uttering curses in Norse, and one or two were uttering curses in English.

"At least it's the last day of the work week," muttered Faolan as he pulled on his boots.

"It is?" asked Cathal. "We get tomorrow off?"

"Of course. Tomorrow is Sunday. Half of Birka is Christian, at least the Norse half." He then walked to the other end of the cabin and asked one of the slaves, "Are you Christian?"

"The name's Gustav, and no, we're not Christian. We're too old to switch faiths. You'll find that most of the younger men and women in Birka converted to Christianity, if only to spite their parents. The older folk can't be bothered with such nonsense."

Faolan shrugged his shoulders and walked out the door, followed by Cathal. One by one, the woodcutters finished dressing and filed out of the cabin and sat around the campfire, waiting on their assignments. As they waited on the foremen, they took turns scooping out reindeer stew from a kettle by the fire.

As he waited his turn in line, Cathal could see Danika carrying a jug of mead. She dropped it off by the campfire, then walked back towards her cabin. He nudged Faolan and asked in a low voice, "Is it Danika's job to prepare the food?"

Faolan nodded as he grabbed a cup and filled it with mead. "That's one of the things she does."

"What else does she do around here?" he asked.

Faolan was about to answer when Domyan kicked open the door to his cabin and stomped towards the campfire. "Alright, everyone sit down and shut up. After I hand out the assignments, you can go back to eating all my food. Cathal!"

"Yes?"

"I want you in the same location, up north." The foreman then pointed towards the slaves. "I want *you* and *you* to help Cathal with the birch trees today. And *you*," he said, pointing at the third slave. "You're to work with Faolan today. The rest of you will be working at your usual assignments." He then spun around and marched back to his cabin.

"What a surprise," muttered Faolan under his breath. "The foreigners and slaves are always stationed up north." He shook his head and muttered a few more Irish curses.

Cathal sat down and started to sip at his bowl of reindeer stew. He was surprised at how tasty the food was. He figured Domyan was a man who would cut costs anywhere possible.

"Breakfast is the best part about this job," said Faolan, as he greedily slurped at his stew. "Danika's cooking is the only thing that pulls me out of bed in the morning. Well, that and Domyan's yelling."

This engendered a few laughs from the loggers.

As Cathal grudgingly finished up his breakfast, one of the slaves sat next to him and said, "Looks like we'll be working together today. Have any advice for an old man?"

Setting his bowl down on the ground, Cathal held up his blistered hands and said, "My advice? Wear wraps on you hands."

"Hell, son. I could have told you that!" the old slave laughed. He slapped Cathal on the shoulder. "My name's Gustav. That's my brother Gottfrid, and that's my other brother Greger," he said, pointing to each in turn.

Cathal leaned forward and curtly waved to each man. As he waved at Greger, he furrowed his brow and asked, "Is he going to be okay?" The old slave was standing there, blankly staring forward and incessantly shaking, as if he were freezing.

"Who, Greger?" said Gustav. "Don't worry about old Greger. It just takes him a bit to get warmed up. Put an ax in his hand and he'll chop down more trees than any three woodcutters combined!"

"I suppose," said Cathal, with a dubious look. He didn't see how any of the three old slaves could last more than an hour chopping wood, and Greger looked like he was about ready to fall over where he stood.

Instead of Domyan storming out of his cabin and shouting at them, it was Mirko who stood up and said, "Alright men, it's that time. Pick up your axes from the tool shed and let's get to work."

The men hurriedly finished their bowls of stew, then set them on the ground. One by one, they grabbed their axes and strolled off in different directions to their assigned locations. Gustav fell in step beside Cathal, with Greger soon falling far behind.

"Is he going-"

"He'll be just fine," Gustav quickly interrupted. "As I said, he just needs a while to get warmed up."

Cathal pursed the corner of his mouth as he looked back at the quickly fading slave. He supposed it wasn't his problem, but if Domyan found out, there would be trouble. After walking for a few minutes in silence, Cathal finally said, "I don't often see slaves your age."

"Ha! I suppose not," said Gustav. "Usually, after a number of years, a slave can earn enough money to pay for his freedom, but my brothers and I have a gambling problem. Every time we have more than a few coins in our pocket, we squander it all away on dice. Hell, we've been slaves for so long that we wouldn't know what to do with ourselves if we ever got our freedom."

"Dice, eh? Tell me, do you know of a fisherman that goes by the name of Old Mats?"

"Of course we know Mats. Hell, my brothers and I would be free men if it wasn't for that old fisherman. That man makes more from dice than he does from fishing!"

After they arrived at the northern logging site, Cathal and the two slaves wrapped their hands with rags and got to work. Cathal's hands pulsed with pain every time his ax bit into the tree. He gritted his teeth and continued on. Such was the life of a woodcutter.

It was hard work; his sore muscles ached and complained. After a half hour, he started to perspire. He leaned his ax against the tree and wiped the sweat from his brow. Looking to his right, he could see Gustav chopping away at his tree. Not bad for an old man, he considered. Turning to his left, he saw Greger just standing there, shaking. The jittery old man was staring into the woods, looking at nothing in particular.

With a brief sigh, Cathal adjusted the straps on his hands and picked up his ax. After a few swings, he turned to Gustav and asked, "What are your thoughts on the wolf attacks?"

Gustav stopped and clenched his teeth. "Damned wolves. Damnable creatures," he spat.

He'd already asked Old Mats about the wolves, but he wanted to see if other Norsemen shared the old fisherman's thoughts. "Rumor has it, the Norsemen are training wolves to kill off foreigners. Once the migrants are all gone, the Norse can reclaim their logging and herding industries."

The slave furrowed his brow. "But there's not enough Norsemen to fill those positions! I may not understand politics, but I'm old enough to see what's going on; it's simple economics. There's not enough workers to fill jobs, so the Norse gladly accept help from migrants. Why would the chieftain want to kill off migrants when there aren't enough workers in the first place? It doesn't make any sense."

Cathal nodded his head; he figured as much. The chieftain had no motive for killing foreigners, and the Slavs had no motive for killing their own workers in the logging camp. That left one of two possibilities: Either the Turks from the reindeer camp were culpable, or the attacks were simply coming from an unusually aggressive wolf pack. But that didn't explain the creature that walked among them. "Have you seen anything strange, other than wolves, out there in the woods?" asked Cathal.

Gustav hefted his ax and said, "No, can't say that I have. I've heard rumors, though."

"What kind of rumors?"

The old slave pursed his lips and started to chop away at the birch tree. "You shouldn't concern yourself with superstitious rumors. Wolves are bad enough."

"Well put," said a voice from behind the two woodcutters.

Startled, Cathal jerked his head around to find Danika staring at him. She was wearing a simple brown apron-dress and was carrying a jug of water.

"I thought you could use something to drink," she said, lifting up the bottle. She then shifted her gaze to Greger, who continued to look forward, staring at nothing. The old slave was still shaking, as if he were a thin tree in a strong storm.

"He's just taking a break. Nothing to get worked up about," said Gustav.

Danika raised an eyebrow and offered a half-smile. The jittery old man amused her. She passed the jug to Cathal, who took a deep drink, then handed it to Gustav. With a thoughtful expression, Danika then turned back to Cathal and said, "Walk with me."

As she walked into the woods, Cathal jogged a few steps to catch up to her. They were heading northward along a faint, leaf-covered trail. Large oak and birch trees towered over them, gently swaying in the wind.

Cathal cast a worried glance into the woods, always on the lookout for wolves. "You're not worried about a wolf attack?" he asked.

With her eyes studying the path before her, Danika looked up in surprise, as if she had not considered the danger. A troubled look then crossed her face. "I was wondering if you were a Christian," she said, ignoring his question.

Cathal paused for a moment, briefly taken back by the change in subject. Was she avoiding his question? Slightly annoyed, he said, "Everyone in Birka seems concerned with what I believe in."

"Of course they are. What you believe in is a reflection of who you are. I was curious, because I wanted to ask a Christian about possession and exorcism."

With raised eyebrows, Cathal turned and gave her a perplexed glance. What an odd thing to say! "I'm no Christian. I simply believe in the natural order of things."

"But surely you must have some faith?" She sounded truly concerned.

Cathal gave a brief, stiff smile. "Forgive me. I'm usually asked that question by judgmental Christians. But you're no Christian, are you?"

She offered him a mischievous smile and said, "What gave you that idea?"

"I suppose the question is, do you worship Veles, as your brother does?"

Danika shook her head and said, "No, I worship the goddess Devana."

"Ah, the virgin goddess of the hunt," noted Cathal. "Quite different from Veles."

"Yes, but then we all tend to worship the gods that reflect our own nature. Or is it the other way around? Perhaps it is the gods that reflect human nature?"

Cathal inwardly smiled; he was impressed. "In answer to your question, I worship the Celtic gods."

Danika gave him a questioning look. "Celtic gods?"

Keeping his eyes warily on the forest around him, Cathal said, "A thousand years ago, the Romans conquered most of the Celtic kingdoms, making it illegal for the Celts to worship their gods and speak their own language. Only in Ireland and certain areas of northern England did the religion survive, and only for a few hundred years. Then, a little over five-hundred years ago, Christianity overtook the Celtic religion in those areas, as well. Many believed that our religion was dead, when in fact, it was simply hidden. The Celtic religious leaders merged with the Christian clergy, and operated from within the Christian church. They have done so for hundreds of years."

"Why would the Christian leaders allow such a thing? Aren't all religions fiercely insular? I find it hard to believe that Christian priests would allow another religion to operate under their own churches and monasteries."

"It's the simplest reason of all – knowledge. The Celtic holy men had a strong oral tradition. They memorized an immense amount of ancient knowledge that was handed down over thousands of years. The Christian leaders had more foresight than the Romans or the Greeks; instead of banning the religion, they appropriated it. They have benefited from Celtic wisdom for hundreds of years, and no one, except a few Christian bishops and priests, have been the wiser."

After walking in silence for a few moments, Danika said, "It seems to be the way of things – new religions supplant the old. We Slavs laugh at the Norse gods, knowing they are but frail imitations of our own gods, and yet the Christian god is slowly replacing both of our religions."

"It is the way of things," admitted Cathal, with a tinge of bitterness. "What interests me are the similarities between all of these different religions."

"What do you mean?"

"Well, take for instance the concept of the world tree – it has a central narrative in the Celtic religion. But the world tree also exists in the Slavic, Turkish, and Norse religions, as well."

Danika stopped and studied the Irishman, squinting her eyes in scrutiny. "You seem to know an awful lot about religion and history, for a doctor."

"Your brother said the same thing." He awkwardly waited a few moments. When she did not reply, Cathal gave an uncomfortable smile and said, "In regard to your original question, I've actually seen exorcisms being performed, back in my home city of Dublin."

"Did the exorcisms work?"

"In a manner of speaking, I suppose. I have a suspicion that some of the exorcisms were successful due to the power of suggestion. In other cases, I believe the possessed just wanted attention. I've never seen an exorcism that couldn't be explained by some other means of logical inquiry."

She had a slightly disappointed, yet far away look in her eye. Danika then brought up her hand and waved off the matter with a laugh, "It's not important. I just thought..."

"Yes?"

She crinkled her brow, searching for the right words. "If Christian priests can exorcise demons from their own faith, do you think they could exorcise demons from the Norse and Slavic religions, as well?"

Cathal narrowed his eyes and jerked his head to the left, not quite sure if he saw something move, just beyond the nearest trees. "I don't know. I..."

"What is it?" she asked.

He whipped his head around, wildly looking in every direction. Something was out there, watching them. He was certain of it. "We need to get out of here."

"I don't see anything."

Without asking, Cathal grabbed her arm and urgently whispered, "Come on!" He then started to run to the south, towards the logging camp, with Danika stumbling after him. They sprinted for several minutes. Trees blurred past them as twigs and leaves crunched under their hurried footsteps. His lungs screamed for air as he raced through the thick wood. Danika was trying to pull her arm away; yelling for him to stop.

Ignoring her plea, he continued on.

And then he saw it. It was standing in the middle of the trail, only a hundred feet before him. An ominous sense of foreboding washed over him, as his vision narrowed to a tunnel.

The creature was hunched over and growling, looking at him with fierce, hateful eyes. It slowly crept forward on four legs, its front legs much longer than its hind legs. It then stopped. It sniffed the air and let out a low roar. It was studying them.

With a horror-stricken gasp, Cathal's hand instinctively clutched at the pouch of wolfsbane that was tied to his belt. He knew that hunters used the poison to coat their weapons...but he had no weapon! Cursing himself for his lack of foresight, he protectively stepped in front of Danika and defiantly stood his ground, though his fortitude was not nearly as strong as his countenance would suggest. He was dumbstruck and nearly crazed with delirium. *This couldn't be happening!*

The beast took another step forward and cocked its massive head to the side. A malevolent grin slowly crept across its black lips, revealing a row of wickedly large teeth. It was playing with them; the type of game a predator would play with its prey. The creature then tensed its body and bolted into the woods; a blur of black fur and claws.

"Run!" choked Cathal, his voice was cracked and strained. After taking a few running steps, he looked back. Danika was simply standing there! In exasperation, he peered into the woodline and said, "Come on. It's stalking us!"

She looked at him as if he were touched. "What's stalking us?"

"The creature! Didn't you see it?"

Her only response was a troubled look. She canted her head to the side and studied him, unsure of what to say.

Cathal scanned the woodline with wild eyes. Did he imagine it? Impossible! The creature was real. He was certain of it.

After a few moments, Danika said, "I think the events of the last few days are starting to catch up to you. My advice would be to not mention this to anyone, lest they think you're insane." Without another word, she walked past him, towards the logging camp.

Chapter 8

With more than a little apprehension, Cathal walked back to his station at the north end of the logging camp. At first, he followed quietly behind Danika. After a few minutes, she veered off the leaf-covered path, into the woods. He watched after her for a moment, then continued on, shaking his head and grumbling to himself.

Did he imagine the creature? In his mind, he went over the incident again and again. While it was true that he was stressed and out of sorts over the events of the last few days, he prided himself on being a man of sound judgment. And yet, the things that recently transpired seemed to have a strange effect upon his mind.

He decided to keep the incident to himself, for now. Cathal was equally distressed by the fact that he confessed his religion to Danika. If anyone back in Dublin knew that he'd spoken of the collusion of the Celtic religious leaders and the Christian church, he would be excommunicated or worse. But he supposed that a handful of Slavic woodcutters halfway across the world wouldn't care about the politics of faraway religions.

It seemed so strange that the violent wolf attacks in Birka seemed mired in a tangled web of religion and superstition. There was a connection to all of it – the wolves, the rumors, the opposing religions...it was all leading to *something*. What that something was, seemed just beyond his grasp.

As he reached his station, he could see Gustav talking with his brother, Greger. Gustav seemed to be telling his brother about some seedy gambling story, while his brother simply stood there and gazed into the woods, shaking uncontrollably.

With a raised eyebrow, Cathal picked up his ax and started chopping away at his birch tree. It wasn't his job to manage the slaves. Besides, he had more pressing matters on his mind.

"Had a little chat with Danika, did you?" observed Gustav.

With an exasperated sigh, Cathal said, "Just get back to work." He didn't want to talk about it.

Gustav chuckled as he picked up his ax and began chopping at his tree. "Getting sweet on the foreman's sister. I'm sure that will end well," he laughed.

Cathal scowled and didn't bother to reply. What was the use of arguing with an old slave?

A few hours later, towards late afternoon, Cathal heard a horn blare in the distance, in the direction of the logging camp. His body involuntarily tensed as he turned towards the sound. "Do you think that was a warning?" he asked Gustav.

"No, that horn signals the end of the workday. Most beautiful sound in all of creation," joked the old slave.

Cathal nodded and turned towards Greger, who was quivering and staring off into the woods, as usual. Since their arrival, the old Norseman hadn't picked up his ax once.

It was a slow walk back to camp, as Greger shuffled his feet in short, faltering steps. His brother held him by the elbow, while telling fishing stories to no one in particular. Cathal could have walked on ahead, but he decided to match their stride, lest they get lost on their way back.

Nearly a half hour later, they came into view of the camp. Most of the loggers were sitting around the campfire, listening to Domyan blow off steam. The foreman was pacing back and forth, throwing his hands into the air in an emphatic manner, yelling at no one in particular.

As the three woodcutters entered the logging camp, Domyan jerked his head in their direction, snorted, then continued on with his diatribe. "Can you believe it? We lose seven men...*seven*! And the chieftain is simply sitting there, playing board games with his daughter! I could tell that he didn't care in the slightest. When I asked him for more workers, he just shrugged his shoulders, as if it weren't his responsibility. The conceit of the man! I tell you that back home in my country, a chieftain is a man of strong moral character. A chieftain is a leader who is willing to sacrifice for his men." He spat upon the ground, then continued, "Any fool can be a woodcutter. Any idiot can be a fisherman or work in the copper mines. Not many people can lead men. Fewer still can lead men into danger. I tell you that the chieftain of Birka is *not* a leader. He is a pretender, and should be deposed."

Cathal quietly took a seat next to Faolan. The two Irishmen quickly exchanged furtive glances, but said nothing. Was the foreman inciting a rebellion, or just blowing off steam?

Noticing the worried glance, Domyan stopped in front of Faolan. A cruel grin creased his lips as he said, "What about you? Do you have the courage to lead men?"

Faolan stiffened. He turned several shades of white and stammered, "I-I'm just a woodcutter."

The foreman's hard countenance softened, as he broke into a laugh. "Just a woodcutter!" His jovial attitude abruptly stopped, as he snarled and slapped Faolan across the face, causing him to fall backwards off his seat. Biter growled and sprang to her feet, ready to defend her owner. Domyan gave the dog a withering, hateful stare, causing the giant wolfhound to take a tentative step back. Cathal then stood up and was about to say something, when Domyan simply pushed him, causing the Irishman to fall backward over the log he was sitting on, landing next to Faolan.

Domyan started to pace around the campfire once again, as if nothing had transpired. "Christians," he muttered. "Damned Christians have no place in this world." As Faolan climbed to his feet and sat down, Domyan rushed towards him and shouted, "Do you think your Jesus is greater than Veles? Do you think your god more powerful than the combined might of the Slavic gods?" He was pointing his finger directly at Faolan's face.

Faolan just sat there, visibly shaking.

"Do you know the problem I have with Christianity?" continued Domyan. "Everything is good or bad, black or white. There's no room for complexity. With only one god, there is only one rigid law, but with a whole pantheon of gods, a man can choose which god suits him. He has a choice. And what is a man without choice?" Domyan shot a glance towards the three Norse brothers, then returned his gaze to Faolan. "A man without choice is a slave, and that is what you are – a slave!"

The entire campsite was deathly quiet, almost comatose with fear.

At that moment, the door to the foreman's cabin squeaked open, and Danika walked out. She was carrying two jugs of mead. She seemed oblivious to Domyan's rantings, as she simply sauntered over to the campfire, handed the jugs to two random loggers, then walked back into the cabin.

Domyan's expression softened, as he regained his composure. He let out a heavy sigh and said, "Drink up, lads. We've all had a hard week. Enjoy your day off tomorrow." He then walked back to his cabin, seemingly deflated. After he shut the door behind him, an audible sigh of relief could be heard across the campsite.

One of the Slavs started playing a lute, plucking the four strings of the old instrument in quick succession. The woodcutters drank and spoke amongst themselves, paying no heed to the foreman's prior rantings, as if his outburst was simply a matter of course.

Cathal turned to Faolan and asked, "Are you alright?"

Rubbing his jaw, Faolan gave a half smile and nodded his head. By that time, the jug of mead had made its way around the campfire. As the man to his right passed him the jug, he took a swig then handed it to Cathal. "Just another average day," he joked.

Nodding his head, Cathal took a drink from the jug, then exhaled loudly. "Just another average day," he repeated.

The next morning, Cathal woke up early, just before sunrise. He raised his head and looked around the rickety old cabin. The other woodcutters were still in their cots, soundly sleeping. One Slavic man at the far end of the room was loudly snoring.

Cathal sat up and put on his boots, then quietly walked out of the cabin, careful not to wake his fellow workers. Once outside, he turned to close the door behind him. Then, from the corner of his eye, he saw a giant animal quickly running towards him. He barely had time to react, when a giant tongue slobbered across his face. "Biter! Knock it off," he admonished.

The wolfhound happily continued to jump and lick his face, as he struggled to push her away. "Okay. Enough, enough," he laughed.

Biter wagged her tail and followed him to the cold remains of the campfire.

After nudging the blackened logs with the tip of his boot, Cathal conceded that he would need to relight the campfire. Luckily, there was a stack of lumber nearby; he needn't waste the morning collecting firewood.

It took him only a few moments to reignite the campfire – the dried twigs and logs spat and sparked, then finally roared to life. He then cast a glance towards the foreman's cabin. He didn't see a light under the door.

With another furtive glance towards the foreman's cabin, he took out his pouch of wolfsbane and poured half the contents into a pan. He then mixed in a half cup of water and a pinch of potato starch as a binding agent. Picking a stick off the ground, he stirred the concoction until it gelled into a thick paste.

Careful not to get any on his hands, he poured the thick poison into an empty pouch and closed the drawstring. If the wolves were upon him, all he would need to do is stick a knife or an arrow tip into the pouch – a mere drop of the poison would stop a wolf dead in its tracks, and if the legends were true, it would kill a werewolf before it hit the ground. With hardened eyes, he gazed into the flames of the campfire. He wouldn't be caught defenseless again.

The sun was just peaking above the horizon as the woodcutters slowly filed out of their cabin. They mulled around the campfire for a bit, warming their hands. After a few greetings and good mornings, they made their way to Birka to spend their hard-earned silver.

"Aren't you going into town?" asked Faolan.

Cathal sat there, unsure. He needed to go into town to pick up more supplies and possibly talk with the chieftain, but he also wanted to go to the reindeer camp and ask the Turks about the wolf attacks. As he mulled over his prospects, he asked, "Is there a way I could get my hands on a bow and a quiver of arrows?"

Faolan scratched his chin and said, "Well, if you're going hunting with the intention of bringing back enough deer meat for everybody, I suppose you could ask Domyan for his bow. Otherwise, you would need to buy one in town."

Grumbling under his breath, Cathal reached to his side and felt the coins in his pouch – he didn't have nearly enough for a bow. Perhaps he had enough for a cheap knife, depending on his bartering skills. After a moment's consideration, he made up his mind to go into town first. He wasn't going to walk all the way to the reindeer camp without a weapon by his side. With an irritable sigh, he asked, "I suppose Danika isn't going to feed us this morning?"

With a laugh, Faolan said, "I'm afraid not. On Sundays, we're on our own."

Cathal stood up and stretched his back. He then slapped Faolan on the shoulder and said, "Alright, then. Let's go to town."

As they walked down the trail towards Birka, Faolan had a hard time concealing a mischievous smile. Finally, he turned to Cathal and said, "So...you and Danika, eh?"

"What?"

"Rumor is, you and Danika are sweet on each other."

Cathal loudly exhaled and did his best to look annoyed. He brought up his hand and waved off the matter. "You heard wrong. All we did was go for a walk in the woods."

With a knowing smile, Faolan said, "That's how it starts! In my experience, there's always a bit of truth to any rumor. So, are there going to be any little Slavs running around here in nine months?"

"Oh, shut up."

The two shared a good-natured laugh as they ambled down the dirt trail.

It was a lazy Sunday morning in Birka. Less than half of the store fronts and booths were open. Cathal wondered why that was, until he noticed a large group of Norsemen standing outside of an old wooden church. It seemed that over half the population of Birka was waiting for morning service to start.

Faolan stopped in front of the church with a conflicted look on his face. He scratched at his beard and said, "I suppose I should go to service this morning."

"That's good old-fashioned Christian guilt talking," said Cathal with a snicker.

"That Christian guilt is the only thing keeping me honest." With a heavy sigh, Faolan added, "You go on ahead. If I don't go to service, I'll feel guilty for the rest of the week."

Cathal nodded and waved farewell. A part of him was curious as to what type of service the Norsemen performed, and how it differed from the service back home in Ireland. He knew there was merit to the Christian god, just as there was merit to the Norse and Slavic and Celtic gods. As a young boy growing up in Dublin, he was forced to go to church, if only to maintain appearances. There was a tremendous amount of community pressure to attend service at least once a week. Most of the villagers in Dublin attended daily.

He exhaled loudly and shook his head. He had a busy day ahead of him. Perhaps next Sunday he would have enough time to satisfy his curiosity.

Feeling a grumble in his stomach, the first thing Cathal did was eat a breakfast of grilled cod and potato cakes at the tavern. He was disappointed that Old Mats wasn't there. Besides Faolan, the old fisherman was the only person he felt comfortable talking to. He wondered where the old man lived. Did he have a family? Or was he simply a lonely fisherman, living out the rest of his days doing what he loved?

After breakfast, he walked outside, placed his hand on his stomach and slightly bent forward. The food from the tavern was playing havoc with his digestion. He wiped the sweat off his brow as he continued on down the street.

Luckily, he was able to purchase a cheap knife at one of the booths. He ran his thumb along the edge of the blade. The knife was sharp enough, and it had a nice handle, fashioned from an elk's antler. He placed the knife in its leather sheath and tucked it into his belt. Perhaps next week he would have enough silver to buy a bow.

Next, he stopped by a booth selling herbs and he refilled his stocks of comfrey leaves, calendula, and wolfsbane. He was surprised to find a measure of mistletoe on display. As he pondered purchasing the herb, Danika's image flashed across his eyes, and a sly grin crept across his face. He pointed to the mistletoe, and had the shopkeeper snap off a portion. He carefully placed all the herbs in separate pouches and tucked them into his belt, right beside his new knife.

Satisfied with his purchase, he set off towards the chieftain's longhouse. Would the chieftain be at home, or at church? He shook his head to clear his muddled thoughts. He then took a deep breath to settle his nerves – that damn breakfast was giving him fits. Was he suffering from food poisoning? Did the tavern knowingly serve spoiled food to migrants?

Muttering a few Irish curses under his breath, he continued on. How much should he tell the chieftain? Would he even grant Cathal an audience? As a foreigner, he had his doubts. He stepped off the main road and strolled down a wide path towards the chieftain's longhouse. Up ahead, he could see a guardsmen standing by the door with his arms folded across his chest.

Raising his hand in greeting, Cathal said, "Is Torsten available for an audience?"

The guardsman cocked his head and scowled, disapproving of the migrant's odd dialect. "The chieftain is at church, as you should be."

Cathal narrowed his eyes, wondering if the guardsman understood the irony of his statement. He decided not to make an issue of it and turned around, back towards the main road. How long did church service last? It had been over an hour since he parted ways with Faolan.

He walked to the north, towards the church. As Cathal approached the old wooden temple, he could hear the muffled voice of the priest conducting his sermon.

Cathal stopped in front of the church for a moment, deciding if he should wait or continue on. As he stood, he listened to the muted words of the sermon, barely audible with the wind whistling past his ears. He heard the preacher describe the tribulations of Jesus, as he wept over the fate of Jerusalem. The messiah knew that in a short while, the city would be torn apart by Roman soldiers.

As he listened to the sermon, he realized that the Christian religion had no reference to werewolves, at least not in the literal sense. When he was a boy, he remembered two monks arguing over Daniel 4:33, a passage that described Nebuchadnezzar, the exiled king of Babylon, as he was transformed into a hideous beast and ran through the forest. One of the monks argued that Nebuchadnezzar couldn't be a werewolf because scripture stated that the beast ate grass like an ox. The monks finally concluded that the insane king of Babylon was merely possessed by a demon.

Cathal pondered the implications of his situation from a religious point of view. It seemed that Christianity, a newer religion, didn't have much to say about werewolves, whereas the Slavic, Norse, and Celtic religions *did* mention the beasts. He had a suspicion that whatever was transpiring here in Birka, was an ancient evil from a forgotten age. Shaking his head, he decided to walk to the Turkish reindeer camp. Maybe they had some insight to this situation.

As he walked down the dusty road, a few biblical passages flitted past his mind. There were more than a few passages in the bible that explained how vicious wolves were. From memory, Cathal quietly recited Matthew 7:15: *Beware of false prophets, who come to you in sheep's clothing, but inwardly are ravenous wolves.*

A rueful smile creased his lips; perhaps the bible *did* have a few things to say about the situation in Birka...

Chapter 9

The reindeer camp was located at the western edge of the island, nearly a half-hour's walk from Birka. As he entered the camp, Cathal received more than a few uneasy glances from the Turks. A quick scan of the workers confirmed the foreman of the camp didn't hire anyone outside of his ethnicity.

The Turks were easy to recognize on sight. Their olive skin, short hair, and close-cropped beards stood in stark contrast to the wild long hair and beards of the Norse and Slavic people. And while most of the Turks dressed in the same drab attire as the rest of Birka, no doubt purchased from the same clothing vendors in town, they liked to wrap colorful scarves and handkerchiefs around their necks and belts.

As Cathal walked towards the campfire, he asked several Turks if they spoke Norse. He received the same suspicious stare and the same shake of the head, no.

"Can I help you?" asked a man sitting by the campfire. He was smoking from a short wooden pipe. The smoke had a strangely familiar scent.

"I'm looking for the foreman," answered Cathal. He felt more than a little uncomfortable amongst the accusing eyes of the Turks.

The man waved his hand in a dismissive manner. "We're not hiring. Try the logging camp," he said, pointing towards the east.

"I *am* from the logging camp. I simply want to talk to the foreman about a few things."

The man cocked his head and narrowed his eyes, scrutinizing the newcomer. He carefully drew on his pipe and said, "You have a strange accent for a Norseman. You're a bit on the small side for a Norseman, too."

Cathal pursed his lips and replied, "I'm an Irishman."

"Ah, an Irishman! Come have a seat by the fire. What can I do for you?" he asked.

Taken back by the man's sudden change in hospitality, Cathal graciously nodded his head and took a seat. The man snapped his fingers, and a subordinate hurriedly fetched a pot of tea that was sitting on a nearby table.

"You're the foreman, I take it," noted Cathal, as he accepted the cup of tea from the underling.

"Call me Firas."

Breathing in the sweet smell of the pipe, Cathal asked, "Can I ask what you're smoking?"

Firas smiled and passed him the pipe. "It's the dried roots of the angelica plant. The Norse call it *angelikarot*."

"Ah, I have a friend in town who smokes the same herb. Do you know a man by the name of Old Mats?"

"Old Mats," Firas nodded his head and offered a grim smile. "Yes, we've lost quite a bit of money gambling with him. He's a good man...for a Northerner."

After Cathal drew smoke from the pipe, he coughed a few times and pounded his chest with his fist. The smoke tasted sweet, if not a bit pungent. He then handed the pipe back to Firas.

"What brings you to my camp today, Irishman?"

"I wanted to ask if you've had any recent wolf attacks."

With narrowed eyes, Firas looked at him suspiciously. "Were you sent here by Domyan?"

"No, I'm here of my own will." Cathal sipped at his tea. It had a strong, bitter aftertaste. "The logging camp had a wolf attack recently. We lost over half our workforce. I was wondering if you've had similar problems."

"Problems? Yes. There's always problems with the wolves – they kill two or three of our reindeer every week. There's no help for it; it's what they do."

"Have they killed any of your workers?"

Firas nodded his head. "Every month or two I lose a worker to those damned creatures. My men know the risks, and yet they stay. Where else are they going to find work?"

Cathal scratched at his neck and looked at the campfire. He was surprised to hear the Turkish camp only lost one worker every month or two, whereas the logging camp had much more frequent attacks.

"Is that why you've come all this way? To ask about the wolf attacks?" asked Firas.

"Partly. There's something else I would like to ask you, but I hope you won't think I'm foolish for asking it."

Firas smiled graciously and said, "You see? This is what I like. Civilized conversation between two men of different cultures. I could never have this type of conversation with a Norseman. They consider all other cultures beneath them."

Nodding his head, Cathal said, "It's the same everywhere. Foreigners visiting any land are treated as second-class citizens. There's no help for it." He then leaned forward and said. "Domyan blames the Norsemen for the wolf attacks, but I can find no evidence of their involvement. I was wondering if you had any thoughts on the matter."

Firas let out a long stream of smoke, then looked thoughtfully at the campfire. "I have more than a few thoughts on the matter, I can assure you of that! In my eyes, the Slavs are to blame for the wolf attacks. They push their logging operations too far into the forest, into wolf territory. The wolves are simply defending their land."

Cathal grew more serious. He leaned forward and asked, "Have you seen anything else in the woods, other than the wolves? Something that moves amongst the pack?"

As Firas puffed on his pipe, he looked down, troubled. "I know what it is you speak of, but I cannot say for sure. I have a notion of what it might be..."

"Yes?"

"I hesitate to say. You see, in our culture, we have legends regarding the relationship between wolf and man."

"Exactly!" exclaimed Cathal. "That's why I came here, to ask you that very thing! You see, in my studies, I have found that every culture has a legend that notes the connection between man and wolf, whether it be Irish, Norse, or Slavic."

Firas paused for a moment, watching the smoke rise from his pipe. He then shifted his gaze to Cathal and said, "There is an old Turkish legend of a boy who was the only survivor of an enemy attack. The rest of his village was slaughtered, and the boy, no more than fifteen years old, was too injured to care for himself. A she-wolf found the boy and licked his wounds. The wolf brought him food to eat and protected him from predators. After a time, the boy recovered from his wounds and grew stronger. A few years later he became a man and took the wolf as his wife. He impregnated the wolf and she gave birth to ten babies. The infants were not entirely wolf and not entirely human, but both! One of the wolf-kin grew up to be a mighty leader by the name of Ashina."

Cathal slowly nodded his head. It was as he expected – every culture had a legend of the werewolf, even the Turks. But even though every culture had a myth that acknowledged the beasts, none of the myths explained *why* there was a connection between wolf and man. For what purpose? Clearing his throat, he said, "The other day, as I was walking through the woods, I came across a creature, half man and half wolf. It was stalking me. It watched me with hateful eyes, then sprinted into the forest. The creature moved almost faster than I could see. Have you ever seen such a thing?"

The foreman of the camp looked troubled. He hesitated for a moment, then said, "Personally, I have not seen this creature, but I have heard rumors. My herdsmen have spoken of such beasts. They refuse to go out and tend to the animals, unless they are in a group, fully armed with bows and axes."

"Beasts? Your men have seen more than one?"

"I am afraid that is correct. According to the herdsmen, there are at least three of those black demons prowling the forest.

Cathal sipped at his last bit of tea and set the cup on the ground with shaking hands.

Three demons? No wonder the Turk's herdsmen insisted on being armed with bows. That would also explain why they lost fewer men to wolf attacks. Odd that Domyan didn't see the need to arm *his* workers with bows.

The Irishman nervously craned his head upward and noted the position of the sun. He then stood and bid farewell. He wanted to get back to the logging camp before dusk.

Before Cathal left the encampment, the foreman offered him one final bit of advice. He looked at the Irishman through a hazy cloud of smoke and said, "For as long as we have walked this earth, we have had a contentious relationship with the wolf. It is in man's nature to push towards the unknown; to expand his territory and conquer new lands. But that expansion always comes with a price, a price the men of Birka are paying dearly for. Remember – in the end, nature always wins."

Raising his hand in farewell, Cathal waved at the Turkish foreman, then slowly walked towards the east, ever vigilant for creatures just beyond the periphery of his vision.

As Cathal entered the logging camp, he saw the woodcutters mulling about the campfire, drinking and talking amongst themselves. They looked up briefly at his arrival, then went about their business, not bothering to greet the Irishman.

Quickly perusing each face, Cathal tried to locate Faolan, without much luck. But he did see Biter sitting dutifully by the sleeping quarters. He walked over to the ramshackle cabin and opened the door, while absently petting the dog with his other hand. The late-day sun crept into the dark interior, as he whispered, "Faolan, are you in here?"

"What? Cathal? Where have you been?" answered a sleepy voice.

Cathal walked into the room and shut the door behind him. "Are you sleeping? It's still daylight out."

Elbowing his way up to a sitting position, Faolan rubbed his eyes and let out a long yawn. "I must have fallen asleep. Too much mead."

"Drinking after church service, eh?" said Cathal with an impish grin.

"Some call it drinking, I call it Irish communion."

Cathal laughed and sat down on the edge of his cot, just opposite of Faolan. "How was church? I came back after an hour, thinking service would be over, but the priest was still giving his sermon."

"Ugh," Faolan lamented. "It was brutal. Service was nearly three hours long! Honestly, I would rather chop wood all day than go through that again. And the singing! The Norse have no ear for music. It sounded like a pack of wild dogs were being slaughtered. The entire time, I imagined god in heaven, clamping his hands tightly over his ears and grimacing in dismay."

"Ha! Glad I missed it."

Faolan scratched the top of his head and said, "So, what did you do today?"

"I walked over to the reindeer camp and had a talk with the Turkish foreman."

"What? Why?"

Cathal shrugged his shoulders and said, "I simply wanted his take on the wolf situation.

Did you know that he gives bows to all of his workers for protection?"

"He does? Maybe I should ask him for a job," lamented Faolan. "What did he say about the wolf attacks?"

"He believes the logging camp is pushing too far into wolf territory; that's why they're attacking. It's clear that he doesn't like Domyan either, for reasons he didn't get into, and he blames the chieftain of Birka for not providing adequate protection."

"Well, I suppose there's enough blame to go around."

Cathal exhaled loudly. "No one knows anything. The Turks are blaming the Slavs, the Slavs are blaming the Norse, and the Norse don't care enough to do anything about the situation. I need to talk to the chieftain and impress upon him the importance of my mission here."

"Your mission?"

Pursing his lips, Cathal cursed inwardly. He then lifted his hands and gently rubbed his temples. He needed to guard his thoughts more carefully. "Never mind," he said warily. "I'm just tired."

Faolan crinkled his brow, but said nothing.

Music started to play outside, coming from the direction of the campfire. From what he could hear, the instruments sounded like a lute and drums. The song was slow and mournful, much like a dirge. Cathal shot a questioning glance to Faolan.

"Every Sunday night, the Slavs like to throw a big party and drink and dance. Since the wolf attacks and all that transpired this last week, I didn't think they would bother."

"It doesn't sound like much of a celebration," noted Cathal. He walked over to the window on the far side of the cabin and propped open the wooden shutters. Peering outside, he could see four of the Slavic woodcutters, plus Domyan and Danika sitting around the campfire. Two of the loggers were playing their instruments, while Danika started to sing a hauntingly beautiful poem. She was sitting on the far side of the campfire, staring into the flames as she sang.

Cathal caught his breath as he watched her. She was such an unusual woman; elegant in manner yet so reserved. He found her absolutely captivating. Her soft voice carried through the evening, beckoning to him. He stood there for a moment, mesmerized by her beauty. Then, from the corner of his eye, he observed a slight movement. Turning his head, Cathal was horrified to see Domyan starting straight at him; the foreman's judgmental eyes seemed to peer into his soul. With a barely audible gasp, Cathal quickly turned away and walked back to his cot.

"Do you think we should join them?" asked Faolan.

"No," Cathal quietly replied. "I think they are mourning their dead."

Chapter 10

The next few days passed by without incident. If nothing else, the blisters on Cathal's hands started to heal. But as his hands healed, his thoughts became more troubled. Images of shadowy creatures clutched at the fringes of his mind, threatening his already disordered sense of reasoning.

Shaking his head, Cathal waved off his encroaching dementia and continue to chop away at his birch trees. As he worked, he kept one eye on the northern treeline. He was almost certain the monster, that half-man, half-wolf beast, was just beyond the trees, waiting for him. Often, he would stop work and jerk his head wildly around at some imagined noise, only to realize a moment later that it was all a fabrication from his addled mind.

At times, it seemed as if the mystery and danger that surrounded Cathal would melt away, and was replaced by a clarity of mind and conviction of purpose. At those times, he was positive that he understood the pieces of the puzzle before him – the connection between the different religions, the wolves, and most importantly, how they all pointed to that dark legend that dwelt in the forest.

He became obsessed with those connections. He meticulously went over the different myths in his mind, piecing together fragments from different histories and different cultures to fill in the gaps. He compared the ancient gods to one another. What were the differences between Perun, the Slavic god of thunder, to Thor, the Norse god of thunder? What were the differences between the Turkish legend of the werewolf, to the Norse and Slavic legends?

During one such moment of contemplation, Cathal put down his ax, turned to Gustav and asked, "What do you know of Fenris?"

The old slave briefly paused from his labors and said, "Fenris is the great wolf, son of Loki, and harbinger of the end times. He will kill Odin, and in turn, be killed by Odin's son Vidar."

Cathal nodded impatiently. He already knew of the myth. He wanted the Norseman's interpretation of the tale. He asked, "What does that mean to you?"

Gustav leaned on the birch tree he was working on and contemplated for a moment. Finally, he said, "The myths are written in such a way that each man can interpret a personal meaning from them. That is why the Norse religion is so much more powerful than Christianity. While the pantheon of Norse gods reflect the nature of man, Christianity merely holds up a perfect deity, and expects man to conform to that impossible ideal."

"But why do you think the end times will be brought about by a giant wolf?"

Gustav shrugged his shoulders. "In the case of Fenris, he is one of three children, born of a wicked father. Of course Fenris grew up to be an unruly wolf and had to be chained – he had the same blood as the trickster god Loki running through his veins. Isn't the son's penchant for destruction a consequence to the sins of his father? It shows that a man is responsible for more than himself, that his own wickedness reaches far beyond his own life, and affects all those around him, especially his children. Fenris, enraged at the world for the simple fact that he was brought into existence, means to destroy all of creation, if only to end his pain and torment from those who would chain him."

Cathal stood there, impressed with the slave's explanation. He found the Norse people quiet and contemplative. They might be outwardly boastful and jovial, yet inwardly they were brooding and forlorn. Was it because of the stark, cold landscapes they inhabited, or something else?

He then looked over to Gustav's brother, Greger, who was still shaking and looking off into the distance. Greger was a quiet man, stoic even. Perhaps he was contemplating mysteries even greater than the riddles Cathal was trying to solve. Peering closer, he could see that the old slave was making smacking noises with his lips and drooling. A two-foot string of spittle was dangling from his mouth.

Perhaps Greger wasn't as contemplative as he first imagined, grinned Cathal.

A sharp whistle, far in the distance, caused Cathal to whip his head around. Peering into the woodline, he could see Domyan, motioning for him to come closer.

"Cathal! Stop lounging around. You're needed back at camp." With that, the foreman turned around and walked back into the woods.

Gustav shot a worried glance at Cathal and asked, "Are you going to be okay?"

"I'll be fine. I'm sure Greger will pick up the slack for me while I'm gone." He offered Gustav a half-smile as he slung his ax over his shoulder. He then quickly walked back towards camp.

When he entered the logging camp, Cathal spotted a curious thing – a large black cauldron sitting on the ground. A huge stack of birch logs was stacked beside it. Domyan was standing beside the cauldron, impatiently waiting for him.

With an agitated sigh, the foreman said, "The chieftain just came by. He placed an order for a couple barrels of tar. Have you ever made tar before?"

Cathal shook his head, no.

"Well, come on then, it's not too hard. Even an Irishman can do it." Domyan laughed as he kicked the black cauldron, causing it to ring like a giant, ominous bell. He then pointed to the stack of logs. "You're going to need to cut those logs into strips, about three inches thick, like this." He picked up one of the logs and, with an ax, started to chop away at it. A few moments later, he had five evenly cut sections of wood, which he neatly stacked into the cauldron. "The trick is to have all these small strips of wood stacked side-by-side, pressed up against each other, so they hold in place. It will take you a few hours to chop all the wood. I've asked Mirko to lend you a hand."

Gritting his teeth, Cathal nodded and hefted his ax. He would rather do this alone, than have to listen to Mirko all day. As he started to chop away at the birch logs, Domyan walked back to his cabin and closed the door behind him. A few minutes later, Mirko walked out of the woods and joined him.

Without a greeting, the Slav sat on an old stump, took off his boots, and started to rub his feet. "Have you ever made tar before?" he asked in his raspy voice, while kneading his toes with his fingers.

Cathal averted his gaze. "Domyan just showed me how."

"So you've never made tar before," Mirko spat. He then put on his boots and stood up. He marched over to the tool shed, grabbed a shovel, then walked back with a smug look on his face. "Just keep doing what you're doing. I'll start digging a trench. With any luck, we'll be done by the end of the day."

"Why are you digging a trench?"

"Just do as you're told, Irishman." Mirko gave him a condescending stare, then started to dig. "If a senior logger tells you to do something, you do it. Why is that so hard?"

Cathal didn't reply. He sighed inwardly. Of all the people he could have worked with, it had to be Mirko.

"I hear you've been sneaking around, asking people about things better left unsaid."

"Sneaking?" asked Cathal, incredulously.

Mirko coughed and spat upon the ground. He grabbed the front of his neck and grimaced. He then scratched at his scar and mumbled a curse under his breath. "The wolves have been a problem for Birka long before you arrived. They'll continue to be a problem long after you're gone. Whatever it is you're trying to do won't help matters. I can assure you of that."

"And what makes you so sure?"

Mirko stopped digging and gave the Irishman a disdainful look. "What is it with you Irishmen? Always imposing yourself on everybody – just like your damned religion. If hundreds of screaming Norsemen from Birka can't solve the wolf problem, then I doubt one skinny Irishman will make much of a difference."

"I'm simply looking for a way to mitigate the danger; to save lives. Did you know the Turks in the reindeer camp each get bows for protection?"

"The Turks? Those idiots?" Mirko laughed, then coughed. "We have axes for protection. If a woodcutter isn't strong enough to defend himself with a good ax, then maybe he should look for another line of work."

"And what about the other creatures that lurk in the woods?"

Mirko cleared his throat and spat once again. "Tall tales made by superstitious men. If there are such creatures, I've never seen them. Dammit!" He stopped digging and clutched at his throat.

Cathal smiled inwardly. He had to admit, Mirko's discomfort brought him a good deal of satisfaction. He wondered if the Slav's nasty disposition was a result from the hanging, or if he was always a miserable son of a bitch.

For three solid hours, Cathal cut the birch logs into strips and placed them into the cauldron. Once the cauldron was tightly filled, they pushed it to the trench and turned it upside down, so it straddled the ditch.

After sticking several handfuls of kindling beneath the cauldron, Mirko lit a fire, then explained, "Once the fire gets hot enough, the wood will start to burn and tar will drip down into the trench and then flow into this recession I've dug out. Every few minutes, you'll need to scoop out the tar and put it into one of these barrels. While you're waiting to scoop tar out of the pit, keep yourself busy by chopping wood for the next batch." He then dropped off his shovel by the tool shed and walked towards the sleeping quarters.

"Where are you going?"

"Mind your own damn business," cursed Mirko in his raspy voice. He then coughed a few times and slammed the door shut behind him.

Cathal didn't protest, he would rather work alone than with the sour woodcutter, even if it meant taking twice as long to procure the tar. He stood there impatiently, waiting for the tar to drip down into the trench. Finally, a thin trickle of gooey black liquid fell from the cauldron. Cathal shook his head in wonder; he never would have guessed that tar was made in such a manner.

After an hour of scooping tar from the trench, the first batch was completed. Cathal had one of the two barrels filled with tar and was chopping extra wood into strips for the second batch. A few hours later, the second batch was complete. Exhausted, Cathal looked at his hands – they were stained pitch black. He imagined that his face looked the same way from all the black tar smoke.

The door to the foreman's cabin creaked open and Domyan stepped out. He was carrying a curved horn, fashioned from a goat's antler. He blew on the horn, signaling the end of the workday. The foreman then walked over to Cathal and asked, "All done?"

Pointing towards the two barrels, Cathal replied, "All done."

Domyan nodded and said, "Good, good. Where's Mirko?"

With no small amount of satisfaction, Cathal pointed to the worker's quarters.

Domyan scowled and marched over to the ramshackle building and stepped inside. A few moments later, Cathal could hear the foreman yelling Slavic curses, as a sleepy-eyed Mirko stumbled out of the building.

Cathal laughed, just as Mirko snapped his head up and bore him a scathing glance. The Slav then clenched his fists and stomped off into the woods. A moment later Domyan walked out of the cabin, looked around, and asked, "Where is he?"

Shrugging his shoulders, Cathal pointed towards the woodline. The foreman simply shook his head and walked back to his cabin.

A few minutes later, the loggers started to enter the camp. They came from all directions, in ones and twos, wearied and worn. Biter then loped out of the woods, followed by Faolan.

Cathal raised his hand to wave a greeting as Biter jumped up and placed his front paws on his shoulders and proceeded to lick his face. The great wolfhound then sneezed, after tasting the awful black tar that encrusted his skin. Cathal laughed and scratched the dog behind the ears.

"You look like hell," noted Faolan.

"That bad, eh?" lamented Cathal. He tried to rub the black tar off his hands with limited success.

"It takes a few days for the tar to wear off," said Faolan.

Nodding his head, Cathal asked, "You've done this before?"

"Of course. The Norsemen use the tar to seal their longships. Every week or two we get an order to make that crap. It's a nasty job, so Domyan usually has the least senior worker procure the tar."

Cathal nodded his head glumly. "Heh, and here I thought he gave me the job because he didn't like me."

"Oh, he definitely doesn't like you," laughed Faolan. "Come to think of it, I don't think he likes anyone."

"Well, I'm sure the feeling is mutual," grumbled Cathal.

The next morning, Cathal rejoined Gustav and Greger at the north end of the lumber camp. He was glad to be out chopping wood again, as he found procuring tar to be a foul, unhealthy assignment.

As two of the men chopped wood, Greger continued to shake and stare off into the distance. Finally, Cathal put down his ax, turned to Gustav, and said, "I don't think your brother has chopped down a single tree since he started here."

"Don't you worry about Greger. If the wolves decide to attack us, you'll be glad he's here."

Cathal looked dubiously at the old slave. "You must be joking. He can barely stand on his own, much less fend off a wolf attack."

"You don't understand. Once the berserker rage overcomes him, absolutely nothing can stop Greger. If you ever saw him fight, you would hold your tongue," spat Gustav.

With narrowed eyes, Cathal looked at the old slave. Greger was shaking like dry leaf in a stiff breeze. He shook his head in exasperation, but decided not to make an issue of it.

Later that afternoon, Cathal started to get an uneasy feeling. It had been eleven days since the last wolf attack. In that time, he'd not so much as seen a wolf lurking in the woods. He wasn't sure if his mind was playing tricks on him, but he was almost certain that he saw a few wolves darting between trees, far in the distance. He asked Gustav if he noticed anything. The old slave simply shook his head and continued to work.

More than a little uneasy, Cathal hefted his ax and walked over to a new birch tree. In the last week, they had cleared quite a few trees from the area, and were pushing farther northward.

The snap of a twig caused him to whip his head around. "Did you hear that?" asked Cathal.

"I didn't hear anything," huffed Gustav. It was getting late, and the old slave was showing signs of extreme fatigue. Every few minutes, he needed to take a break to collect himself.

Snap. There it was again!

With wild eyes, Cathal scanned the forest around him. Nothing. Far off in the distance, he heard the sound of Domyan's horn, signaling the end of the work day.

"It's about damn time," muttered Gustav.

At that moment, Cathal saw a pack of four black wolves charge out of the treeline, racing towards them. He gripped his ax with white knuckles, frozen with fear. Behind him, a bony hand grasped his shoulder as Gustav leaned in and said, "Not to worry! Greger will take care of those pups."

Cathal whipped his head around and gave Greger an incredulous stare. The old man, who not two minutes ago was shaking like a leaf, held his ax high above his head and was shouting war-cries to Odin!

Greger then sprinted forward, yelling like a man possessed.

With a laugh, Gustav slapped Cathal on the back. "Now you'll see some real action!" the old man bellowed. "My brother's specialty is killing wolves!"

Cathal watched in awe, as Greger sprinted right into the midst of the pack and swung his ax at the largest wolf. The wolf nimbly jumped to the side, causing the old man to miss and stumble forward. The three other wolves then jumped on the Norseman's back, tearing into him with wild abandon. Cathal involuntarily shuddered at the sound of crunching bones, as the wolves bit into the slave again and again. Greger screamed out in pain as he was dragged to the ground, with chunks of his flesh ripped from his frail body.

With crazed eyes, Gustav pulled at Cathal's tunic and screamed, "Run!"

Chapter 11

Cathal and Gustav ran as fast as their legs could carry them, as the sound of snarling and torn flesh faded into the distance. After a few minutes, Gustav fell to his knees and began sobbing. The old man was too exhausted to continue on.

"Just leave me here," he sobbed. "I don't want to live in this world without my brother."

Cathal grabbed him by the shoulders and pleaded, "Get up, get up!" He then turned his head towards camp and screamed for help.

Clenching his jaw, he tugged and dragged the old man down the trail as best he could manage.

After a few moments, Cathal stumbled and fell. Cursing his luck, he quickly regained his feet. That's when he saw it – a dark form emerging from the woods. It was hunched over and snarling, loping towards them with a malicious sneer on its black face. The beast seemed to stared into his soul.

Cathal felt a scream rise from his chest, but he heard no sound. His mouth was open, screaming, but the world around him seemed silent and still. It was as if he were locked in a horrific nightmare, bound in place, awaiting his inevitable demise.

The beast was thirty feet away from him and closing fast, when an arrow streaked past Cathal's ear and thudded into the werewolf's chest. The creature reached up and ripped the arrow from its body and tossed it disdainfully to the ground. The beast roared hatefully at Cathal, then turned and bounded into the woods.

Cathal started to babble incoherently. The stress from being almost torn apart, in addition to seeing Greger ripped limb from limb, was too much for him. He rolled over and clutched at the earth, grabbing handfuls of dirt and leaves as he chanted Celtic litanies over and over.

With a disgusted scowl, Domyan shifted his leg back and kicked him in the side. "Get up," he growled. When Cathal continued to chant and clutch at the earth, the foreman reached down and dragged him to his feet, shoving him forward. "Run, you coward!" he yelled.

Finally, Cathal regained enough of his faculties to stumble forward. He could see Gustav running ahead of him, with his bony knees raised comically high in the air. With the foreman pushing him forward, Cathal was finally able to break into a run. A few minutes later, they were back at the logging camp, doubled over and gasping from exhaustion.

Danika was standing by the campfire with a fierce look in her eyes. "What happened?" she asked.

"What do you think? Another damned wolf attack," spat Domyan. He notched another arrow in his bow and carefully watched the northern treeline.

Gustav was on his hands and knees, sobbing uncontrollably. "Greger is dead! My dear brother is dead!" he repeated over and over.

"Well, I doubt that will make much of a difference to our bottom line," laughed Domyan.

Danika rushed to Gustav's side and tried her best to console the slave. She then shot her brother a scornful glance and said, "Stop acting like a goat's ass and do something!"

"What am I to do?" growled Domyan, as he continued to scan the woods.

As the siblings argued, Cathal glanced over towards the campfire, were several of the woodcutters were gathered. Most of the Slavs were nervously looking about, unsure of what to do; all save for one. Mirko returned Cathal's gaze with a roguish grin.

They recovered Greger's body a few hours later. Half his corpse was missing; the sharp edges of gnawed bones stuck out of his body at precarious angles. His right leg and arm were gone, as was half of his face. Greger's one remaining eyeball gazed blankly at the darkening sky above him.

After they buried the body in a clearing to the east, the loggers slowly walked back to camp. The two remaining Norse brothers stayed at the gravesite, mourning their loss. They quietly stood by the grave, solemnly bowing their heads and whispering prayers to their gods.

Once they were back at the campsite, most of the men started drinking right away. They sat around the fire, watching the flames and smoke reach silently towards the stars, as they ruefully passed a jug of mead amongst themselves.

"To hell with this," said Cathal, as he stood up and marched towards the south.

"Where are you going?" asked Faolan, as he stood up and hurried after him.

"The chieftain needs to know about this. He needs to *do something* about this. I'm not just going to sit around while the wolves pick us off one by one. Domyan refuses to do anything about these attacks. Who else am I to turn to?"

"Don't be a fool," pleaded Faolan. "The chieftain doesn't give a damn about us."

"No, but he *does* care about his own kind. Slave or not, Greger lived in this town for decades, and with two of his guardsmen dead from the previous attacks, the chieftain will need to take action, unless he wants a riot on his hands."

Faolan grabbed his arm. "Stop and listen to reason. The chieftain isn't going to listen to you. I doubt he'll even grant you an audience."

Cathal gritted his teeth and said, "He'll grant me an audience once he learns who I am." With that, he wrenched his arm free of Faolan's grasp and continued to storm down the trail towards Birka. After a few minutes he glanced behind him. He was disappointed to find that Faolan did not follow him.

With a weary sigh, he continued onward, down the dark trail.

"He's not here," said the guardsman with a tired yawn.

"Well, where is he?" asked Cathal impatiently.

"Where do you think? He's at the tavern, where he is every night."

Cathal let out an irritable sigh, then turned around and stomped off towards the tavern.

"You're wasting your time, Irishman," the guardsman called after him.

As he stormed away, Cathal lifted his hand and waved the guard off in a dismissive manner.

The tavern was not far; he could already hear the clank of cups and silverware and rowdy patrons singing off key. As he approached the front door, a drunken Norseman stumbled out, bent over and barfed on the ground in front of him. The man then righted himself on unsteady legs, smiled a toothless grin, then stumbled back into the tavern. *Wonderful*, thought Cathal, as he pursed his lips and stepped over the puddle of yellow and brown vomit.

He opened the door to find the tavern teeming with rowdy, drunken Norsemen.

Music was playing in the back of the room, as three men, who could barely play their instruments, plucked and strummed their lutes and patted their drums. One Norseman was standing on the center table, singing to the discordant tune. Cathal almost did a double-take. The man standing on the table was Torsten, the chieftain.

With a disgusted snort, Cathal walked up to the chieftain and tried to get his attention. He stood there for a moment waving his arms. When he wasn't noticed, he reached up and grabbed Torsten's leg.

One of the Norsemen from the crowded room roughly nudged him and said, "You do *not* touch the chieftain!"

Cathal took a step back. The Norseman was nearly a half-foot taller than him and was obviously looking for a fight. Shaking his head in frustration, Cathal walked to an empty table and took a seat. He would need to wait for the right moment to approach the chieftain.

He sat glumly and impatiently tapped his fingers on the table. Every few moments, some drunken idiot would bump into him, then walk off without an apology. Cathal didn't know what was worse – Torsten's horrible singing, the band's lack of musical ability, or the *smell* of dozens of unwashed halfwits packed into the small tavern.

"Can I take your order?" asked a portly barmaid.

He sat there for a moment, deciding if he should stay. Finally, he held up two fingers, signifying two cups of mead. The barmaid pursed her lips then walked off, quickly vanishing into the throng of rowdy patrons.

Cathal couldn't get the image of Greger's mutilated body out of his mind. The way those wolves tore through his flesh and snapped his bones as if they were twigs... He shuddered involuntarily. He then dipped his head down and placed the palms of his hands on his temples. He squeezed his eyes shut, trying in vain to cast out the disturbing images that permeated his distraught mind.

"We're out of cups," said the barmaid.

He opened his eyes to see the waitress holding two drinking horns. She shoved both horns in his direction, which he awkwardly accepted with both hands. She then walked off without another word.

With a heavy sigh, Cathal started drinking from one of the horns. There was nothing he could use to hold the drinking horns upright on the table, so he sat there and drank the contents down as quickly as possible. A short while later, the barmaid came back and he once again held up two fingers.

A couple of hours later, and the Irishman was thoroughly sloshed. At least a dozen drinking horns littered the surface of his table. They rolled and jumped every time one of the drunken patrons bumped into the table. Cathal was so inebriated, he didn't even mind. He could barely remember why he came here in the first place.

Then it hit him. The wolves. And that damnable creature! He snarled and slammed his fist down on the table, causing several of the drinking horns to jump and roll off the edge, clanking to the floor below. At that point, Cathal was beyond caring about any of it. He came into the tavern with something to say, and by the gods, one way or another, that damn chieftain was going to hear him out!

Cathal stood up and attempted to climb onto the table with unsteady legs. He swayed to and fro, almost falling over. Steadying himself, he slowly stepped onto the chair, then made an exaggerated step onto the table. Success! He grinned foolishly as he bent over and picked up two of the empty drinking horns. He then straightened himself into a full standing position and shouted, "I have something to say!"

The uproarious crowd barely acknowledged him, as they continued to grunt and sing and have a merry time of it. Not to be ignored, Cathal stomped his boots on the table and yelled, "There is a demon amongst you! Half man and half wolf!"

The music abruptly stopped, as the crowd of drunkards settled down and looked at him with suspicious eyes.

"Not three hours ago, the wolves killed another man. A Norse slave, by the name of Greger." He could hear a few gasps from the crowd. Good. In a small town such as this, everyone knew everyone else. "At the north end of the logging camp, the wolves came and ripped Greger limb from limb! He's now lying in a shallow grave while you are frolicking about, oblivious to the danger that surrounds you."

The tavern was completely silent now. He had their undivided attention.

"Last week a total of nine men died, including two guardsmen, and no one did anything about it. Will *you* sit here and do nothing? Are you but sheep, waiting to be slaughtered?" Cathal then took the two drinking horns and held them to his forehead. With his bloodshot eyes and tar-blackened skin, he looked as if he were a crazed demon. He looked over the drunken crowd with accusing eyes. "*You* know of the demon that stalks these woods. The demon commands the wolves, inciting them to attack! And if you do nothing...if you just sit here like the miserable lot of sheep you are, the demon will come for you!"

The crowd of patrons stood on their feet and screamed at Cathal, enraged beyond measure. How *dare* a foreigner talk to them in such a manner! A few of the rowdy Norsemen started throwing half-filled cups of mead at him. He tried his best to protect himself by covering his head with his forearms.

Sensing the mounting danger, Cathal attempted to step down from the table. Then, from the periphery of his vision, he saw a large object careening through the air towards him. Before he had time to react, a chair smashed into the side of his head, knocking him off his feet and onto the floor. The last thing he saw

before he lost consciousness, was a large group
of angry Norsemen forming a circle around
him.

Chapter 12

As he opened his eyes, Cathal could see the sturdy crossbeams of a vaulted ceiling overhead. He was lying in a comfortable bed, with a wool blanket pulled up to his chest. He tried to sit up, but the throbbing in his head caused him to reconsider.

Cathal slowly raised his hand and felt the side of his head. He then looked at the tips of his fingers...blood. His head was bandaged and blood was seeping though the fabric.

"I like the way you stopped that chair with your head," joked the chieftain. "In Birka, we duck when things are thrown at us. But to each his own."

Cathal let out a soft groan and lightly touched his head once again. It was swollen and sensitive to the touch, but he didn't think his skull was fractured.

"The völva said to not pick at your wounds."

"I'm a doctor," mumbled Cathal.

"Eh, a doctor? So you're a woodcutter, a drunkard, *and* a doctor? What an industrious group of people you Irishmen are," boasted Torsten. "I might also add that you're an instigator, provoking the good people of this village."

"The good people of this village are being murdered on a regular basis, and you're doing nothing about it."

"Watch yourself, Irishman," said Torsten. "If I hadn't intervened at the tavern, you'd be dead by now. We Norsemen don't like being lectured to by outsiders."

Despite the throbbing pain in his head, Cathal managed to elbow his way up to a sitting position. "Surely you know there is something in that forest; something other than wolves."

"I've never seen such a thing," spat Torsten. "Those rumors are made by frightened men; men who don't have anything better to do than spread gossip. And I keep Birka safe enough – within the town limits, we haven't lost a single person in months. It's only the industries to the north – the woodcutters and herders that are having problems with the wolves. By all accounts, it's *their* problem to deal with."

"I tell you that if *you* don't deal with this problem soon, the wolves will overrun Birka, and this settlement will be but a memory."

"Know your place, migrant. The only reason I saved your worthless hide is because we have a shortage of loggers, and Birka has quotas to fill."

"Do you really think a doctor would risk his life as a laborer for a few coins? The rumors of what have been transpiring here have reached all the way to Ireland. The church has taken notice, and sent *me* here to investigate."

The chieftain narrowed his eyes and said, "What are you getting at? Ireland has no power here. From what I understand, half of Ireland is under Norse rule!"

"Politically, yes. But there is one institution that transcends political boundaries."

Torsten let out a weary sigh; he was beginning to see what the Irishman was getting at. "The church."

"Yes. There are active trade routes between our two cities. More than a few Viking traders came to our shores with tales of demons stalking Birka. The church took notice and sent me to investigate." Cathal only gave the chieftain part of the truth. There was no need to complicate matters by telling him of the collusion between the Celtic religious leaders and the Catholic church. It was the Celtic council that insisted on the investigation.

The chieftain shook his head in consternation. To think that Ireland had a hold over any Scandinavian settlement was laughable, but the power of the church was another matter entirely. Christianity had a firm hold on the region. "And if I refuse to cooperate?"

"I have already sent word of what I've found here. I fully expect an envoy to arrive within the month, but I'm afraid they will arrive too late. We must act now! You're full cooperation will not only be appreciated, but compensated as well."

Torsten's ears perked up. "Compensated, eh?"

"You know how wealthy the church is. They can compensate you for any damages or loss of life, but only if you cooperate. Think about it – *nine* men died last week, and another Norseman was ripped apart just this afternoon. How many more deaths will it take before Birka erupts into anarchy? Help me quell this threat now, and I'll make sure the church rewards you for your efforts."

The chieftain was stubborn, but he was also a practical man. He leaned back in his chair and folded his arms across his chest. "What do you suggest?"

"Gather a large group of men – guardsmen, fishermen, loggers, any volunteers you can find. Put a bounty on each wolf, one silver each."

"One silver each? That's outrageous!"

Cathal held up his hands before him and said, "One silver each, which the church will gladly compensate you for. Think of how many people will volunteer! We can send out a large hunting party tomorrow morning and take care of this threat once and for all. And if we also find the monster that lurks in the woods, so much the better."

Scratching the side of his chin, Torsten finally relented. "Alright then, but in addition to one silver per wolf, I want twenty silver for each man that I lose."

"Done," agreed Cathal.

The chieftain opened the front door and briefly spoke with his guardsman. He then shut the door and said, "Get some rest Irishman, for tomorrow we hunt."

The next morning, a large group of nearly fifty Norsemen gathered outside the chieftain's longhouse. As Cathal looked over the group, he saw a few familiar faces, most notably Old Mats, Faolan, and his wolfhound, Biter.

However, he did not see anyone else from the logging or herding camps.

Walking towards Faolan, he raised his hand in greeting and asked, "Is anyone else coming? I'm surprised Domyan isn't here."

Faolan shook his head, "I think the wolf attacks have affected the Slavs more than they let on. They've lost more than anyone else and want no part of this. Domyan said there's no way he would hunt side by side with the Norsemen. He even let me borrow his bow for the hunt. He told me to have fun and to bring him back a wolf pelt."

Cathal heard the chieftain clear his throat. He turned around to see Torsten holding his hands high above his head, trying to get everyone's attention.

"Alright, listen up," said the chieftain in a loud, commanding voice. "We're going to start at the western coast of the island, and work our way north from there. Be careful not to shoot any reindeer, or any Turks for that matter."

That brought a few good-natured chuckles from the crowd.

"Quiet down," the chieftain spat. "Once we get to the northern part of the island, we'll fan out and make our way eastward, killing as many wolves as we can. Remember, it's one silver per wolf. And don't steal anyone's kill! Let's be civil about this; there's plenty of wolves out there for everybody. Okay, let's move out. The sooner we get this over with, the better."

The Norsemen fell in behind the chieftain in a loose, staggered formation. They were relaxed, almost jovial, enjoying the prospect of the morning hunt. Cathal was more than a little worried. He fell in behind the Norsemen, towards the back of the formation and stared at the ground, brooding. He was startled when a large, rough hand clapped him on the shoulder.

"No bow, eh?" said Old Mats.

Cathal smiled and held up his knife. "No, I like to do my hunting the old fashioned way," he said, with more than a little sarcasm. As he looked around, he could see that most of the Norsemen were well equipped with bows, knives, and axes.

"You Irishmen are a strange lot," laughed Old Mats. "If things get precarious, just stand close to me. I've killed more than a few wolves in my time."

"I appreciate that," agreed Cathal.

The hunting party made their way to the western edge of the island and worked their way northward. As they walked, the Norsemen joked amongst themselves, confident in their strength of number. However, the farther north they trekked, the quieter they became.

Cathal turned to Old Mats and asked, "How large is this island?"

Mats scratched at his neck and pondered for a moment, then said, "Oh, it's about four miles east to west, and seven miles north to south, by my estimation."

"And how many wolves do you think are on the island?"

Shaking his head, the old Norseman said, "That's anyone's guess. Most of the islands along the coast have wolves and bears on them, though how they get there is anyone's guess. Though if you're twisting my arm for an answer, I suppose there's at least fifty to a hundred wolves up north."

Cathal furrowed his brow. That was a lot of wolves for such a small island, but then again, it wasn't the wolves that worried him the most. He shuddered as the image of that monstrous beast flashed across his mind, its amber eyes reflecting pure hatred and rage. That blasphemous creature that only wanted to bring death to those who would encroach upon its territory. He remembered the words of the Turkish foreman, who stated there were *three* such demons on the island. Cathal shook his head. Could that be right?

They were at the midpoint of the island now, still working their way to the north. The herding and lumber camps were to the east, and the ocean was to the west. They saw a few dozen reindeer grazing in the open fields, and even a couple of herdsmen, who nervously watched them as they ambled past.

A few minutes later, Cathal heard one of the Norsemen shout a warning. "There's one!" he yelled. The hunter ran forward, with a few of his companions running nervously behind him. They quickly fell behind, as they eyed the dark woodline with apprehension. The wolf deftly ran behind a cluster of trees, far in the distance.

"Stay with the group!" the chieftain yelled, admonishing the overzealous hunter.

The hunter grabbed an arrow and notched it in his bow, he then carefully pulled back on the drawstring and let loose. The arrow whistled through the air, only to thunk into the ground, far short of the retreating wolf.

"Good shot, Olaf!" laughed one of the men. This was followed by many jeers and catcalls from the Norsemen.

Olaf scowled and offered his companions a crude gesture. He then walked to retrieve his arrow.

"I said stay with the group!" yelled the chieftain once again.

Shaking his head in agitation, Olaf turned around and stomped back towards the hunting party.

Suddenly, a half-dozen wolves sprinted out of the forest, towards the lone Norseman.

Shouts of warning rang out from the hunting party as Olaf turned and looked over his shoulder. When he saw the wolves running towards him, he froze in terror for a moment, then started running towards safety. Several arrows flew past him as he ran, as several hunters were trying to cover his escape.

"Stop shooting, or you'll hit him!" yelled the chieftain.

The wolves were clever – they attacked from behind, using Olaf as a shield to cover their approach from the rain of arrows. They happily yipped and growled as they closed in, only seconds from their prey.

"Dammit!" cursed the chieftain. There was no way Olaf would make it to safety in time. Torsten drew his bow and let an arrow fly, which arced past Olaf's head and slammed into the lead wolf. With a yelp, the wolf tumbled to the ground, dead.

Before the chieftain could get off a second shot, another wolf lunged and bit Olaf in the left leg, causing him to spin and crash to the ground. The five wolves swarmed on the unfortunate Norseman, attacking him from all sides.

"He's as good as dead. Don't just stand there. Fire!" yelled the chieftain, as nearly every Norseman in the hunting party let loose their arrows.

A cloud of missiles descended upon Olaf and the five remaining wolves. The small area around Olaf looked like a bloody pincushion, as man and beast alike were skewered to the ground. One of the wolves was only hit with two arrows. It quickly scampered into the forest. Olaf and the four remaining wolves weren't as fortunate.

Rushing to the fallen Norseman's side, the chieftain and the rest of the hunting party slowed to a walk as they approached the grizzly scene. Olaf was splayed on the ground with over a half-dozen arrows sticking out of him. He looked blankly at the sky with dead eyes.

"What a goddamn catastrophe," muttered Torsten. With a heavy sigh, he then said, "I need two volunteers to drag him back to town. Better yet, drag him to the herding camp and see if the Turks have a cart."

More than a few Norsemen volunteered. Torsten absently picked the two men who were closest to him. He then turned and addressed the crowd. "We aren't hunting rabbits here. Some of you idiots are acting as if this is your first hunt. Stay quiet and stay alert." He then shook his head and muttered under his breath, "Odin's hairy balls, what a mess."

The rest of the hunting party watched in silence as the two men dragged Olaf's bloody carcass to the reindeer camp. Amid the blood and perforated bodies of the five dead wolves, Cathal could see Olaf's discarded bow lying on the ground. It was snapped in two, useless. *Of all the damned luck*, he lamented.

"Alright, let's head out," spat the chieftain. The group cautiously trudged northward, with their bows half drawn. They were apprehensively looking into the forest and snapping their heads at the slightest sound. They were agitated and nervous; a far cry from the jovial mood they were in just a few minutes ago.

One tense hour later, they found themselves at the far northwestern edge of the island. Torsten turned to the hunting party and said, "As we move eastward, keep your eyes peeled. Make no mistake – this is wolf country. There's no telling how many of those damn creatures are out there, so keep an arrow cocked at all times. And I don't need to tell you to stick together. In a few hours from now, if all goes well, we'll be back at the tavern telling tall tales and spending our hard-earned silver on watered-down mead."

This caused a few grins and nods of agreement. What happened to Olaf was an unfortunate blunder. They were alert now – a force of forty-five hardened Norsemen armed with bows and axes.

As they moved eastward, the chieftain instructed the men to fan out in a staggered formation. They slowly crept forward, their eyes darting left and right.

Keeping his eyes trained on the trees ahead of him, Cathal thought he saw movement. He turned to Faolan and asked, "Did you see that?"

"I saw something," whispered Faolan. He then nervously cleared his throat.

"There, up ahead!" yelled one of the Norsemen, as he fired an arrow.

This caused at least a dozen agitated Norsemen to release their arrows into the forest, hitting nothing.

"Hold your fire. Don't waste your arrows," growled Torsten.

At that moment, a dozen wolves raced out of the forest from the south, flanking them.

"To your right! Fire!" yelled Torsten, as another volley of arrows showered upon the wolves. The wolves stopped and raced back into the woods, with three of their number slain.

Several of the hunters let out a whoop, confident they were finally getting the upper hand on the creatures. "That's a total of eight wolves dead!" boasted one of the Norsemen.

Cathal had an uneasy feeling in the pit of his stomach. It felt as if something ominous was overhead, looking down on him. He then looked upwards, through the branches, at the noonday sky. The moon shown directly overhead, dimly reflecting the light of the sun.

While the hunters adjusted their formation to face the south, Cathal squinted his eyes and looked to the east. He witnessed several wolves darting between the trees, then his eyes widened in horror as three-dozen wolves sprinted from the woodline towards the unsuspecting Norsemen. He pointed his finger and shouted, "To the east!"

As the hunting party collectively turned to the left, drawing their bows, Torsten noticed another line of wolves creeping out of the shadows, to the south. An astonished looked washed over his face when he realized what was happening. They weren't the hunters – *they* were being hunted! He let out a stuttering curse, then shouted, "They're boxing us in. Retreat!"

With the shoreline to the north, and wolves to the south and east, they had only one direction to retreat: to the west. In a disorganized clatter, the Norsemen stumbled and sprinted westward, with the chieftain bellowing after them to maintain formation.

In less than a half minute, the chaotic retreat came to a faltering halt, as the men skidded to a dead stop, incredulous as to what they were witnessing – a line of nearly a hundred wolves to the west, panting and pawing at the ground. Standing several paces in front of the wolves was the black-furred demon, hunched over on all fours, growling and gnashing its teeth. It briefly stood up on two legs and let out an ear-shattering roar, signaling the wolves to attack.

The panicked hunters let loose their arrows into the approaching pack.

Unfortunately, less than a dozen wolves fell under the hail of arrows, and the few arrows that struck the werewolf were grasped by the creature and ripped from its body with contempt. The creature then sprinted towards them with blinding speed, easily dodging arrows with preternatural quickness. As the monster barreled into the hunter's front line, it gnashed and clawed, sending twisted bodies careening through the air.

The wolves from the south and east raced to join the fray. The hunting party was completely surrounded, with the werewolf in their midst, swiping and biting all those who were unfortunate enough to get within range. The men were in a complete state of panic; there was no hope of escape.

Dropping their bows and hefting their axes, the Norsemen tried to form a defensive circle, with their backs facing each other. They held their axes before them, ineffectually swinging and jabbing their weapons at the wolves, only to have the creatures faint and lunge at them with wild abandon. One by one, the hunters were dragged from the circle and into the woods, screaming.

The wolves continued to bite and yip in a frenzy of chaotic glee.

Cathal could see Torsten race towards the werewolf with his ax held high. The chieftain let out a mighty bellow as he swung his weapon and buried it deep into the monster's side. The fiend casually backhanded the chieftain, sending him careening to the ground, unconscious. It then wretched the ax from its side and cast it contemptuously to the ground, as a spray of blood erupted from the ghastly wound. The monster paid no heed to its injury, as it loped towards the still body of the chieftain, with a glint of malicious finality in its hateful eyes.

Just as the werewolf reared back to deliver the killing blow, Biter lunged forward and jumped on the monster, sinking her teeth into the creature's upper arm.

Momentarily distracted, the werewolf grabbed Biter by the scruff of the neck and tore her away. The wolfhound ripped out a chunk of the monster's flesh as she was pulled away. She struggled and snapped as the werewolf held her body aloft by one hand. The werewolf then swiped at Biter with its free hand, causing a huge bloody gash across the dog's side. Blood sprayed into the wind as the wolfhound let out an anguished yelp. The werewolf then tossed Biter to the side and stepped towards the chieftain.

As the wolfhound hit the ground, she rolled and crumpled to a stop. Her chest was rapidly rising and falling in a series of struggling, shallow breaths. Cathal could hear Faolan scream. The Irishman ran to his dog's side then fell to his knees. He was crying in anguish, oblivious to the bloody chaos surrounding him.

Cathal held his knife defensively before him as he gazed at the carnage to his left and right; it was complete pandemonium. After only a few minutes, the wolves had decimated nearly half their number. He could see men being dragged across the forest eaten. He could hear the hunters screaming as they were being feasted upon. Cathal felt a mixture of panic and despair, certain these were the last few moments of his life. He dropped to his knees and stared blankly before him; his body in shock from all he had witnessed. It was then that his hand brushed against the pouch that was tied to his belt...the wolfsbane!

With fumbling hands, he wrenched the pouch from his belt and tore open the drawstring. His fingers were madly shaking as he poured the poison onto the blade of his knife. Then, discarding the pouch, he stood up and clutched his poisoned weapon with white knuckles. Before him, not ten paces away, was the werewolf, closing in on the still-unconscious body of the chieftain.

Steeling his nerves, Cathal bolted towards the monster with his knife held high above his head. Just as the werewolf tensed its muscles to lunge towards Torsten, Cathal swung his knife downward, burying it deep into the creature's back.

The werewolf stiffened, then turned around, its eyes wild and drenched with malevolence. It stepped towards Cathal and roared, causing the Irishman to fall to his knees in abject terror. The creature then took another step, faltered, and crashed to the ground, only a few inches from where Cathal was kneeling.

Cathal was shaking and hyperventilating, overcome with dread emotion. He brought his hands up before him, incredulous as to what he'd just accomplished. He then gazed at the beast, it's limbs were still twitching.

The werewolf then turned its head and looked directly at Cathal. There was no recognition in its eyes, only pure hatred. A moment later, the beast let out one final spasmodic twitch, then lie still, its dead eyes staring blankly forward.

As soon as the great beast expired, the wolves stopped yipping and howling. They backed away, seemingly confused as to where they were. The wolves then raced into the forest, leaving the broken and battered Norsemen behind.

Amid the cries of injured and dying hunters, Cathal heard Faolan's wretched sobs. He was kneeling over Biter, the wolfhound's giant head resting on his lap. As he gently petted her, he whispered repeatedly, "It's going to be okay. It's going to be okay..."

Cathal crawled over to him and rested his hand on Faolan's shoulder. "It's over. Biter saved the chieftain's life."

"It doesn't matter," cried Faolan, pushing Cathal's hand away. "She's dying. She's the greatest friend I've ever had and she's dying."

Cathal studied the giant gash in the wolfhound's side. It was bleeding profusely, several bones in the dog's rib cage were broken, and the animal could barely manage shallow, halting breaths.

The wound looked grim, but no major organs appeared to be damaged. He exhaled loudly, trying to determine if the animal could be saved. Regardless, if he didn't act soon, Biter would bleed out.

He glanced at his friend. The pained expression etched on Faolan's face was all it took to make up his mind. "Did you forget?" said Cathal, with an encouraging smile. "I'm a doctor. I can fix this."

Faolan looked up, almost disbelieving.

Cathal took out the hook and fishing line he kept in his pouch and started stitching the wound. His quick, practiced fingers nimbly stitched the wound closed. He then cut the line with his teeth and tied off the end. The animal still needed further attention – it needed a cast and a litter should be constructed to drag Biter back to town, but the dog was stable; she was going to pull through. As Cathal finished, he turned to Faolan and said, "I think she's going to be just fine. You weren't bit, were you?"

In a daze, Faolan shook his head, no. He then broke down into a wretched series of weeps and wails, overcome with emotion. "Thank you," he whispered, as he bent over and frantically stroked Biter's head. "Thank you."

Lightly touching him on the arm, Cathal said, "I need to attend the others." He then stood up and quickly walked to the nearest Norseman lying on the ground. He knelt down by the man and opened several other pouches that were tied to his belt, containing healing herbs and tinctures. He then looked up briefly, surveying the grizzly, blood-drenched battlefield. Over half their number were dead or wounded.

Chapter 13

Cathal was beside himself with anxiety. Most of the men he treated were bitten by wolves, and he knew that most of the wolves carried the infection that caused the frothing disease. As he stitched and mended wounds, his shaking hands were drenched with their blood – infected blood. Nevertheless, he continued on, diligently trying to save as many patients as possible.

After operating on a half-dozen men, he walked over to his next patient – a hunter whose leg was badly mangled and profusely bleeding. Cathal bent over and examined the wound. Blood was spurting out of his leg in rhythmic pulses. He shook his head and scowled. He would not be able to save the leg.

Cathal took the hunter's ax and raised it over his head. Then, gritting his teeth, he swung the ax down as forcefully as he could, right above the hunter's knee.

The hunter tensed and screamed, then passed out. He was breathing in hurried, shallow breaths. Cathal mumbled a curse as he ripped a strip of cloth from the man's discarded pant leg and tied a tourniquet around his bloody stump. He then bowed his head and squeezed his eyes shut. The adrenaline from battle, the horror of almost being killed, and the gruesome wounds he was working on, had an accumulative effect upon his mind. He forced himself to take deep breaths, trying to steady his rattled nerves.

Just when he thought he was getting a handle on the situation, Cathal heard an alarmed shout at the other end of the battlefield. He looked over his shoulder to find a gathering of Norsemen circling around the dead body of the werewolf. They were talking amongst themselves in an unnerved manner.

Cathal stood up and approached the gathering, wondering why they were in such an agitated state. As he walked closer, the Norsemen noticed his approach and let him through. What Cathal then witnessed didn't make any sense: There lie Mirko, dead on the ground, with a knife sticking out of his back. His dead eyes were still open, blankly staring forward.

"That damned woodcutter was the beast," mumbled one of the Norsemen.

Mirko? Cathal was just as surprised as anyone else. Then something tugged at the back of his mind. He furrowed his brow in contemplation. That scar on Mirko's neck – he remembered Domyan mentioning that Mirko was hung by a group of Irishmen. Cathal knew the legend of the werewolf was alive and well in Ireland. People who were suspected of lycanthropy were tied to a post and burned alive, or hanged...

Cathal scratched his chin and pondered the possibilities. Perhaps Mirko changed into a werewolf as he was being hanged? He shook his head; they would never know. But there was still another matter left to consider – the Turkish foreman said there were *three* black demons in the woods. If that were true, then their work had only begun.

The chieftain had able-bodied men construct stretchers to carry the dead and wounded back to town. As Cathal tended to the injured, he could hear the clattering of axes chopping down branches to construct the litters. It didn't take long to realize that they didn't have enough people to carry the dead and infirm, so the chieftain instructed one man to run to the Turkish camp to get more help.

"How are you holding up?" asked Torsten.

Cathal looked up from his surgery and wiped his brow with the back of his wrist. "I'm fine. I wasn't injured in the attack."

Nodding his head, Torsten said, "I want to thank you for what you did. One of my guardsmen told me what happened – how you risked your life to save my own. You've shown real courage, as much as any Norseman. I owe you my life."

Cathal offered a grim smile. He knew the men he was operating on would soon be dead from the frothing disease; it was only a matter of time. Hell, *he* might be dead within a week. Uncomfortable with the chieftain's praise, and morbidly mulling his own fate, he decided to change the subject. "After I killed the werewolf, the wolves seemed disoriented, as if they were under some sort of spell. A few moments later, they stopped attacking and ran into the woods."

Torsten narrowed his eyes and considered the Irishman's words. He then shook his head and said, "Never mind all that. The beast is dead, though it cost us gravely."

"Yes," whispered Cathal, as he bent his head down and continued stitching together his patient. He had a nagging suspicion that there was more to this infernal puzzle, something just beyond his reach. The words of the Turkish foreman continued to ring in the back of his mind – *There are at least three of those black demons prowling the forest...*

As the chieftain walked away to tend to other matters, Cathal saw something move far in the distance. He looked up and slowly scanned the forest around him. Then he saw it – a single wolf with black fur, casually looking at him with curious, almost beckoning eyes. It then averted its gaze and loped off into the woods.

Several hours later, the hunting party had constructed enough stretchers to carry the wounded and dead back to Birka. Over a dozen Turks from the herding camp arrived to lend a hand. They were more than cooperative, and carried their heavy burdens without complaint.

Cathal was happy to see that Old Mats made it through the attack unscathed. Looking over the gathering of Norsemen, he counted a total of fifteen men who were uninjured, including the chieftain and Faolan.

"You are the hero of the day, eh?" beamed Old Mats, as he puffed on his pipe.

"I suppose so," answered Cathal. "Although I don't feel heroic. I approached the beast from behind and struck him in the back."

"And if you didn't, the chieftain and everyone else would have died. Don't worry yourself over such things. Battles are chaotic; anything can and will happen."

Cathal offered the old fisherman a grim smile, but did not reply. He was bothered by too many questions. He knew that Mirko hated him, but the werewolf never singled him out. There was no recognition in the beast's eyes when it gazed directly at him. And to tell the truth, he saw no hint of humanity in those monstrous eyes, only hate and rage. Yet the werewolf did not hunt or kill the wolves. In fact, it seemed to somehow control them. He remembered the look the black wolf gave him, before it loped off into the woods. There was something else to this puzzle, just beyond his grasp. He was certain of it.

It took over four hours to drag the injured and dead back to town. With aching backs and feet, they set the stretchers down in front of the infirmary, then collapsed from exhaustion. As they sat on the ground, amongst the injured and dead, the nurses and the old völva rushed out and started to tend to the injured.

Cathal remembered the old völva. The woman refused to give him a needle and thread on account of the fact that he was a migrant. He shook his head and let out a long sigh; that seemed so long ago.

"There's the man of the hour," said Torsten, as he took a seat on a stump, next to Cathal. The chieftain leaned forward and said, "Six-hundred and forty-two silver, by my count."

"What?" asked Cathal.

"We lost a total of thirty men – twelve dead, and another eighteen men as good as dead. They'll die soon enough from the frothing disease. At twenty silver per man, that's six-hundred silver. Plus and additional forty-two silver for the wolves we killed."

Cathal sighed and canted his head downward, looking at the ground before him. "You'll get your money."

"Damn right," said Torsten. "That money goes to compensate the families of the men we lost in battle."

Cathal narrowed his eyes. He was fairly certain that half the Norsemen here in Birka didn't have families. They were here simply to earn some silver, then move on to the next lucrative job, wherever that might be. "A representative from the church of Dublin should be here in a few weeks."

"Good. After we get this situation sorted out and the injured are in the infirmary, come visit me in my longhouse. We have matters to discuss." The chieftain then stood up and made his rounds, talking with the injured Norsemen.

Other matters? Cathal furrowed his brow. What other matters could he possibly be talking about? Something bothered him about the chieftain's manner – he didn't seem overly concerned with the men who fell in battle. Perhaps that was more a sign of the times than any lack of empathy on Torsten's part. They were working in a dangerous frontier town where the only motive was profit, after all.

What concerned Cathal the most, however, was the fact that over the last few months, Mirko was content with killing his own people – the Slavs of the logging camp. He never made a full-scale assault on the Norsemen until they invaded *his* territory. There was something to that behavior; something more animal than human, but he wasn't quite sure what to make of it.

Cathal stayed at the infirmary for a time, helping where he could, though the old völva and the other nurses paid him no heed. Just as well, he mused. He had no desire to integrate with these people, in this cursed land of wolves and dark gods.

He spent the remainder of his time tending to the Norsemen's wounds and helping the injured to their cots inside the infirmary. As he was finishing up, he noticed Faolan quietly sobbing over Biter.

"What's the matter?" asked Cathal. "Did the stitches come loose?"

"No," said Faolan, in between sobs. "Biter will eventually die from the frothing disease. Then I'll have nobody." He gently stroked behind the dog's ears.

"Were there any other bites or scratches on her body?"

"I don't think so. No."

Cathal offered him a reassuring smile as he knelt down and patted Biter on the rump. "I think she'll be fine. Mirko didn't have rabies."

Faolan looked up with a gleam of hope in his eyes. "That's right! I hadn't even considered." He looked incredulous, with a foolish smile spreading slowly across his lips. "Thank you. Thank you so much."

As the sun began to set, casting long shadows across Birka, Cathal made his way to the chieftain's longhouse. The guardsman at the front door nodded and let him in, which was a far cry from the disdainful tone the man had for him before the hunting expedition.

"Have a seat," said Torsten, as he motioned towards a large oaken table.

Cathal eyed the chieftain carefully. It seemed that Torsten had spent the last couple of hours drinking. He could see his troubled, bloodshot eyes and reddened nose, and his slightly unbalanced posture as he swayed back and forth.

The chieftain sat heavily behind the table, where several half-empty jugs of mead and overturned cups were haphazardly scattered about. "Help yourself," he said, as he absently pointed at the jugs of mead. He then grabbed the cup closest to him and drained its contents. It seemed that the day's events affected Torsten more than he'd initially let on.

After carefully pouring himself a cup, Cathal took a few measured sips and said, "Not bad."

"Eh?"

"The mead. It's not bad."

"Ha! Yes, it's the good stuff. This is a celebration, to mark my conversion," the chieftain slurred.

Cathal narrowed his eyes. "Conversion?"

The chieftain burped loudly and waved off the question. He set his cup heavily down upon the table and stared at his guest with watery eyes. "Something about your story doesn't add up."

"What do you mean?"

"You say you're a doctor *and* a messenger from the Church of Dublin...that makes no sense. I've been a Christian for over ten years, and I've never heard of such a thing. I've heard of missionaries traveling to the far corners of the earth, spreading the word of the gospel, but you've never once mentioned your faith. That's very unusual for a messenger of god – they usually can't stop talking about Jesus."

Cathal stiffened. What was the chieftain getting at?

"I've never heard of a Christian doctor making money from selling his services to heathen religions, either; unless they were on a mission."

"I never claimed to be on a mission," said Cathal.

"Hmm." The chieftain looked at Cathal with suspicious eyes. "Tell me truthfully, is there an envoy coming from Dublin with my silver?"

"Yes. As I said, you'll get your money."

"Then what is your position in the Church of Dublin?"

Cathal let out a heavy sigh. The accumulation of the day's events were starting to wear on him — the wolf attacks, the dying men, and the possibility that he might have contracted the frothing disease sent him to a dark, despondent place. "I'm not a member of the clergy, but I *am* a member of the church," he said guardedly.

"How so?"

Cathal brought up his hand and rubbed the bridge of his nose with his thumb and forefinger. He closed his eyes for a moment, then said, "Before Ireland converted to Christianity, the people worshiped the old gods. Our gods were older than the Norse and Slavic gods, they were perhaps the oldest, most powerful gods ever known to man. We had worshiped those ancient gods for thousands of years before we converted to Christianity. Our traditions and beliefs held *true* power – far greater than the Christian church was willing to admit. The problem facing the church was twofold. One – our holy men didn't keep those thousands of years of ancient knowledge written down. That knowledge was passed down through an oral tradition. And two – the church, zealous though it was, understood that abolishing our religion would destroy thousands of years of accumulated knowledge. So instead of destroying our order, the Christian church silently integrated our religion into its own, allowing *our* religious leaders to continue on with our traditions, in exchange for sharing knowledge."

The chieftain leaned forward in his chair and said, "You're not a Christian, then?"

"No," Cathal admitted. "I'm a member of the ancient order that came before our lands converted to Christianity."

"Which is?"

Cathal paused for a moment and considered his circumstance. He'd already admitted far more than he should have; he was under an oath of secrecy that forbid divulging information about the council *or* their collaboration with the church. Finally, he shook his head and said, "I need your assurance that what I say next, never leaves this room."

The chieftain straightened in his chair. "You have my word."

After taking a deep breath, Cathal slowly exhaled and said, "Over one thousand years ago, the Celts ruled most of Europe and Britannia, but that was quickly changing. The Romans aggressively expanded to the north, slaughtering our people by the hundreds of thousands. They wiped out entire cities and did their best to destroy all traces of our religion and customs. They pushed us to the north, until eventually the Celts inhabited only Ireland and northern England. There the Celts made their last stand, it was a stalemate that lasted for hundreds of years. One of the Roman emperors even built a wall – Hadrian's Wall. The wall divided our land in two. To the north of the wall were the Celts, to the south, the Britons and Romans. After the Romans fell from power, Christianity swept over Europe. The Celtic religion that was once repressed by Roman gods was now repressed by the Christian god. However, the Christian clergy were more open-minded than the Romans. As I said before, instead of destroying every last trace of our religion, the Christian bishops and monks integrated our holy men under the very roofs of their own churches and monasteries."

"And what were those holy men called?" asked Torsten.

Cathal looked at the chieftain with weary eyes and said, "The druids."

The chieftain canted his head and gave him a sidelong glance. "Are you one of these druids, then?"

Shaking his head, Cathal said, "I'm not yet a full druid. It takes twenty years to learn the oral traditions – the myths, the medicines, and the histories. The druids must memorize a mountain of information. They are judges, philosophers, historians, and doctors. In addition, they are the caretakers of the most ancient knowledge that man has ever known."

"How long until you become a full druid?" asked Torsten.

Cathal let out a weary sigh. "A few more years. They save the most ancient secrets and knowledge until the last year. It is then that I will become a full druid and be accepted into the Council of Thirteen. Until then, the council sends me on these investigations to prove my worth."

"And that is why you are here now?"

Nodding, Cathal took another sip from his cup. "Yes, to investigate rumors of lycanthropy. You see, the Celtic religion has known of werewolves for thousands of years. The Norse, Turkic, and Slavic religions also mention lycanthropy in their myths. The druids have a great interest in these beasts, for reasons I'm not quite certain. But whenever a rumor reaches the shores of Ireland, you can be sure the druids will investigate, no matter where in the world the rumor originated from."

The chieftain laughed and pounded on the table with his fist. He then raised his cup high into the air and said, "A toast, then. It appears that neither one of us is Christian."

Cathal furrowed his brow and asked, "How do you mean?"

"Isn't it obvious? We just suffered the worst wolf attack in the history of Birka. The Christian god has abandoned us. I have implored Odin to let me back into his fold, for this is a problem only the old gods can solve."

"I don't understand. We might have suffered horrific losses today, but we *did* manage to dispatch the werewolf."

Torsten looked intently at Cathal with haunted eyes; eyes that had seen far too much pain and sorrow. He then leaned forward and said, "I've always had my suspicions about that logging camp. Domyan in particular. You see, the wolf attacks didn't start until *after* those migrants came to our shores. Since then, year-by-year, the attacks have gotten worse. Not only have the rumors escalated, but sightings of the beasts as well, and I happen to know for a *fact* that there's more than one werewolf out there."

Chapter 14

That night, Cathal slept in the chieftain's longhouse. Since it was discovered that Mirko was one of the werewolves, there was no telling how Domyan might react. Would the foreman deny any knowledge of Mirko's metamorphosis? Would he plan an all out attack on Birka? Unfortunately, their hands were tied; they simply had no evidence that Domyan had any connection to the wolf attacks.

Finally, it was decided that Cathal would stay with the chieftain until the matter was settled, or until the envoy from Dublin arrived in Birka; whichever came first. They came up with the excuse that, because he was a doctor, Cathal was needed at the infirmary due to the large influx of patients. This would allow him to freely visit the logging camp without suspicion.

The matter weighed heavily upon Cathal, as he realized the stakes were much higher now. Domyan was now aware that the entire town held him under suspicion. *What would the foreman do*?

The next day, as they formulated a plan to protect the town, the chieftain suggested a raid against the logging camp – a preemptive strike, before Domyan could mount an attack against Birka.

"I'm not sure the creature would do such a thing," said Cathal.

"Why not? The werewolf just tore into fifty of the most able-bodied men in Birka. Could you imagine the destruction those beasts would cause with a surprise attack in the middle of the night?"

"Wolves are highly territorial. I think the reason they attacked us yesterday was simply because we were trespassing. And if you look at the attacks before yesterday, the werewolf was killing other Slavs, *not* Norsemen."

"What are you getting at?" asked the chieftain.

Cathal canted his head to the side, searching for the right words. Finally, he said, "We might be overthinking this. I believe the werewolf has a hatred for man and man alone, regardless of race. I believe the creature hunts the closest, easiest target, as any predator would do."

"Fine, let the damn beasts wipe out the entire logging camp, for all I care," mumbled Torsten, throwing his hands in the air. He then shook his head and said, "All I can do is increase security and wait for another attack. There's no way the men of this town would volunteer for another hunting party. They certainly aren't afraid to die in battle, but dying a slow death from the frothing disease is less than an honorable way to go."

"We need a way to draw the creatures out."

Torsten shook his head. "I leave it to you to come up with a plan, for the gods refuse to give me any guidance. They silently judge me from above. Perhaps Odin is punishing me for worshiping the Christian god." He then looked at Cathal with haunted eyes and said, "Beseech your ancient gods, and find a way to rid this island of those damnable creatures once and for all!"

Cathal was more than a little apprehensive from the heavy burden placed upon him. As their meeting concluded, he walked out of the chieftain's longhouse and marched his way towards the center of town. He should restock his supply of herbs, and perhaps visit the infirmary, but first he needed to visit the logging camp. Faolan was still at the camp, and he feared for his safety.

He trudged northward towards the logging camp with a mounting sense of dread. The fear he had of Domyan conflicted with the feelings he had for Danika. What if she was a part of this? What if the whole camp was a pack of werewolves? What if Faolan was the werewolf, and he recently bit Mirko, making Domyan and the rest of the Slavs innocent? There were too many questions, and he realized that what he didn't know, could get him killed. He was walking into the camp blind.

As he approached the logging camp, he saw Domyan standing by the campfire. A reindeer was strung upside down from an overhead branch, a steady stream of blood was pooling beneath it. The foreman was diligently cutting away at the carcass.

Cathal cursed himself for his stupidity. He should have walked around the campsite, avoiding Domyan entirely. It was late morning now; Faolan would be at his post, chopping trees at the northern edge of camp.

With his back facing him, Domyan said, "You're late for work, Irishman."

Dammit. Too late. Cathal involuntarily stiffened and said, "The chieftain asked me to stay at the infirmary to help with the wounded."

"Why? They'll all be dead soon," said Domyan, without a trace of emotion. "That means I'm down two more men – you *and* Mirko. Did the chieftain mention anything about reimbursing me for two more workers?"

"No."

"Of course he didn't!" snarled Domyan, as he stuck his knife through his belt, then proceeded to rip the reindeer's hide off with his hands. He pulled the hide downward in stiff, jerking motions.

Cathal involuntarily swallowed and said, "Twelve men died yesterday, and an additional eighteen men are lying in the infirmary. Birka is in a state of panic, and you're worrying about your bottom line?"

"Fretting about what can't be controlled, doesn't pay the bills," snapped Domyan. "Due to the loss of income from the decimation of my workers, I'm forced to hunt, simply to feed my own people!" He then took the knife from his belt and proceeded to saw the head off the reindeer. Halfway through his labors, he turned and flashed Cathal a malicious grin. "Why are you here, then? Come to see my sister?"

"N-no," stammered Cathal, as he tried to maintain an assured countenance. He swallowed once again and said, "I need to talk to Faolan."

"Faolan's busy," Domyan retorted. "You're not trying to take away another one of my workers, are you?"

"Of course not. I simply need-"

"Go back to your infirmary, doctor," Domyan interrupted. "Lest I skin you next." He took a threatening step towards Cathal, casually spinning the bloody knife in his hand. Behind him, the reindeer's head dangled from a thin stretch of muscle, slowly spinning in place.

With faltering footsteps, Cathal stumbled backwards. He then turned around and ran back towards town, floundering over the uneven dirt path.

"You're a coward, Irishman!" Domyan yelled after him. "A damnable coward!"

Cathal pressed forward, running as fast as his legs would carry him. Werewolf or not, Domyan was a deranged lunatic. After a few moments, he chanced a glance behind him. Luckily, the foreman wasn't following. He slowed his pace as he gasped for air. That was the last time he would visit the logging camp, he promised himself.

The quarrel with Domyan bothered Cathal more than he cared to admit. He had no doubt the foreman could come after him at any moment; hunt him like that damned reindeer. And what could he possibly do about it? He was no hunter or warrior. He was a scholarly man, simply investigating a curiosity. He shook his head in dismay. It would take at least three more weeks until the envoy arrived from Dublin. Was he to wait and do nothing until then?

He clenched his jaw and attempted to steady his nerves. No, he would take action. He would show the council that he could take initiative and resolve matters on his own terms, no matter the apprehension he felt.

When he finally reached town, he turned and marched towards the booth that sold herbs and tinctures. He had depleted his stocks, tending to the injured Norsemen. After greeting the merchant, Cathal pointed to the herbs he needed – comfrey, calendula, elderberry and wolfsbane, among others. He pursed his lips; the chieftain should be paying for this. His lips then creased into a grim smile. He should have asked Domyan for his last two days of pay.

After purchasing the herbs, he walked back to the chieftain's longhouse. The place was deserted. Just as well, he mused. What he was about to attempt, required his undivided attention.

He sat at the table and spread the herbs out before him. He also placed a jug of water and a jug of mead beside him. He would need to procure a pure alcohol extract from the mead, to concoct the proper tincture for the poison he was planning to make. He then walked over to the hearth, located in the middle of the longhouse, and suspended the jug of mead over the flames. While the mead came to a boil, he searched the longhouse for as many cups, pans, and containers as he could find. He then let out a long sigh. This was going to take a while.

He grabbed a pan and poured in some water. He then proceeded to pinch a mixture of various herbs into the water as he swirled the pan to and fro. As the water simmered and evaporated over the flames of the hearth, he added in additional herbs, and then poured the alcohol extract into the mixture.

Several hours later, he had a small vial filled with poisonous liquid. He shook his head; all that work for such a small amount. Luckily, all he would need to ingest was one small sip a day. With any luck, he would build up a tolerance to the poison after a few days.

He held up the small vial in front of him and loudly exhaled; it was now or never.

Cathal brought the vial to his lips and sipped, then shuddered violently. As he finished, his whole body shook and convulsed. His lips and the tips of his fingers became numb, and he started to sweat. Sickly red splotches appeared on his skin as he clenched his eyes shut, willing the pain to go away. After a few minutes, the nausea subsided and his breathing returned to normal. *By the gods, what a foul concoction!* Cathal sat there, shaking, his pupils mere pinpoints. After a few more minutes, the painful symptoms receded to a manageable level.

As Cathal cleaned up the mess of plates and pans he'd scattered around his work area, he staggered and swayed. The poison upset his balance and caused his mind to wander and lapse. He thought he saw faint lights, just outside the periphery of his vision, but as he snapped his head around, nothing unusual could be seen. Cathal clenched his jaw and tried to steady his nerves. *It's just the poison*, he assured himself. In a few days, if all went as planned, the symptoms should dissipate.

An hour later, the chieftain walked into the longhouse with his daughter. Cathal was seated by the hearth, shivering and clutching his sides.

The chieftain's affable nature turned to one of concern, as he noticed the red splotches on Cathal's sweat-drenched face. He asked, "Are you alright? You look like death warmed over."

"I'll be okay," mumbled Cathal. He then remembered the food poisoning he acquired from the tavern a while ago. It was as good of an excuse as any, he surmised. "I'm not accustomed to the food here."

Torsten grinned and said, "Ah, the lutefisk! That takes a while to get used to." He then pulled up a chair to the hearth and was about to say something when he looked around, crinkling his nose. "What's that smell?"

"I was procuring some medicine for the patients at the infirmary," lied Cathal. He didn't want to tell the chieftain about the poison. Not yet, at any rate.

"Well, if you must, do that nonsense at the infirmary. I don't want my daughter breathing in these fumes."

Cathal nodded and whispered an apology. It was all he could do to keep the nausea in the pit of his stomach.

"Have you given further thought as to how we'll take care of our little problem?" asked Torsten.

"I've given it much thought, and I'm beginning to formulate a plan, though I will need more time to consult with the gods. Give me one more day, and I will have the answer. I am certain of it."

Torsten looked satisfied. "Good! I will hold you to it then. I don't know if you've been out amongst the populace, but the entire town is frightened beyond measure. The Christian priest is spouting some nonsense about this being the end times; that god is punishing us for our heathen ways. And the völva at the infirmary is implying something else entirely – that the Norse gods are punishing the people of Birka for turning against them and worshiping the Christian god. The entire town is accusing each other for this mess, and if I don't do something soon, we're going to have an uprising on our hands." He then leaned forward and said, "You have one day to come up with a plan. If we wait any longer, they'll be rioting in the streets."

Through a cloud of delirium, Cathal stared back at the chieftain and said, "Since I arrived at Birka, I've been piecing together this mystery. I've been able to connect and contrast the parallels between different myths and religions, and I assure you they all point to the same answer. A few more prayers and meditations and I will have my final solution. One day is all I will need."

The chieftain left Cathal to his meditations. Luckily, the physical ailments he was suffering through diminished greatly by the end of the day.

After imbibing the concoction on the second day, he felt as if he were starting to build up a tolerance to the poison. No longer was he suffering from the cold sweats, nausea, or ugly red splotches across his skin. However, instead of suffering physical ailments, the poison continued to have an accumulative effect upon his mind.

Sometimes he would see strange phantoms appearing from the fringes of his addled mind, and other times he would hear sounds that couldn't possibly have occurred. On numerous occasions, he would ask the guardsman stationed at the front door if he heard a particular noise, only to have the Norseman furrow his brow and look at him with concern.

On the other hand, there seemed to be a strange benefit from taking the poison, at least from his muddled perspective. There were moments of extreme clarity, where he knew that his chosen gods were smiling down upon him. Cathal became certain that he understood the pieces of the puzzle before him, and how they all pointed to the dark legend that dwelt within the forest.

Towards the end of the second day, Cathal sat in front of the hearth, wrapped in a wool blanket, despite the warm summer weather. He nodded his head more than a few times and said, "Yes, of course." Then he would smile and chuckle to himself. Sometimes he would raise his hand and wave it before his face, as if shooing away some bothersome insect, yet there was nothing there. But despite his odd mannerisms, there was a stern conviction in his eyes.

The front door swung open and the chieftain strolled in with a weary countenance. Shaking his head, he grabbed a chair and pulled it next to the hearth, opposite of Cathal.

After wiping his brow with the back of his hand, Torsten said, "I hope you have your plan ready. The people of Birka are increasingly agitated, and there are rumors of insurrection!"

Cathal smiled and said, "The gods have granted me wisdom; they have shown me what must be done."

The chieftain leaned forward. "I'm listening."

With his eyes shining in a blaze of fervent devotion, Cathal straightened in his chair and said, "There is an ancient evil that has pervaded the cultures of the known world for thousands of years. This evil has been around since the dawn of man. No, even further back – this evil has permeated this world since the dawn of the predator. Do you think man is the originator of evil? What a laughable concept! Man was preceded by the gods, and the gods were preceded by the titans. The gods suffer the sins of the titans, just as man suffer the sins of the gods. We wail and reach our hands to the sky, beseeching the gods for deliverance from this evil that surrounds us, and yet the gods have remained silent to our prayers. Do you know why?"

The chieftain looked back at him, through the flames of the hearth, and said, "It is because we have forsaken the old gods, in favor of this new, upstart religion."

"Yes! That's exactly it!" said Cathal excitedly. His hands were shaking, almost jittery, yet his eyes were focused. "There are so many similarities between the ancient religions. Did you know that the Tree of Life is a central symbol in Turkic, Slavic, Celtic, and Norse religions?"

Torsten shook his head, no.

"It's true!" said Cathal, almost too loudly. He then stood up and cast off the blanket he'd wrapped around his shoulders. He bent down next to the hearth, and with his forefinger started to draw the picture of a tree on the dirt floor of the longhouse. "Let's take the Slavic religion, for instance – the religion shared by Domyan and the rest of the Slavs at the logging camp. You see? Up here, at the top of the World Tree, is where Perun resides. Perun is the god of thunder, same as Thor. In the Celtic religion, Taranis is the god of thunder. They reside up here, above the tree of life." He waved his hand above the drawing of the tree.

"What are you getting at?" asked Torsten, narrowing his eyes.

"Hear me out. Hear me out." Cathal was almost maniacal in his enthusiasm. It was clear the poison was having more than a small effect upon his mind. "Below the Tree of Life are the roots, reaching all the way down to the underworld. In the Slavic religion, this is where Veles resides. Veles is the evil one; he despises Perun. The two gods have been locked in conflict for thousands of years, just as Thor and Loki have been!" He looked up to make sure the chieftain was paying attention.

Torsten edged forward in his seat, with a perplexed look in his eyes.

Shaking his head, Cathal said, "Don't you see? The evil comes from Veles – the same god Domyan worships. The same god he has been praying to since he arrived on this island! That is where the evil is coming from."

"What are we to do?"

Cathal stood up and beamed with pride. "We must show the *true* gods that Birka is worth saving. We must show them our conviction is strong! The only way to do that is through sacrifice. If we sacrifice enough people to the god of thunder, then he will strike down Veles, lifting the curse upon this town."

"But we can't sacrifice Norsemen to a Slavic god. That's sacrilege!"

"You won't be. Tell the people of Birka that the sacrifice is to Thor. Don't you understand? Perun, Thor, and Taranis are one and the same – they are the same god of thunder, interpreted by different cultures. Once we give him the offering he awaits, the curse upon this island will be lifted."

"And what manner of sacrifice are you suggesting?"

"I propose we sacrifice the eighteen men in the infirmary, the ones who are tainted with the frothing disease. They will be dead by the end of the week anyway. Their burnt flesh will let the god of thunder know of our conviction."

Torsten leaned back in his chair and scratched his chin. "You're certain of this?"

Looking directly into his eyes, Cathal said, "I have never been more certain of anything in my life. It will take three days to construct the effigy. At the end of the third day, we shall have our ritual, and this nightmare will be over."

The chieftain, wracked with guilt for previously abandoning the old Norse gods, nodded his head in agreement. In his mind, it was the only way. As the flames of the hearth reflected in his eyes, he said, "Let it be done."

Chapter 15

A flurry of activity commenced the next morning, as Torsten ordered every able-bodied Norseman to assist in constructing the enormous effigy. Oak planks that were reserved for the construction of longships were instead used to build the sacrificial statue. The construction took place near the shore, halfway between Birka and the fishing docks. Cathal could hear the workers madly sawing and hammering away at the project from the chieftain's longhouse.

Several times a day, Cathal would walk down to the construction site and oversee the worker's progress, often with a critical eye. "No! Each leg needs to be wider – at least three feet wide, ten feet tall, and hollow!" he would yell at the exacerbated workers. "Think of each leg as a long cylindrical cage. Do you understand?"

The foreman of the project would scratch his head and nod an affirmation, though he was more than a bit dubious as to what Cathal was asking. But he was under strict guidelines from the chieftain to follow the Irishman's orders, so he reluctantly agreed.

By the end of the first day, the construction of both legs of the effigy was complete. As they stood, reaching towards the sky, Cathal craned his head back and admired it's beauty; the structure was proceeding just as planned. In another two days, the effigy would be ready.

"What in the hell is going on?" asked a familiar voice behind him.

He turned around to see Faolan and Biter, each with a curious expression on their face. Cathal stepped forward, and with a gracious smile, hugged his friend. "Isn't it magnificent?" beamed Cathal, with a peculiar hint of madness glinting in his eyes. He then held Faolan at arm's distance and said, "It is a monument to the old gods; a shining beacon of our devotion. It will be the most glorious effigy ever offered to Taranis."

A worried look crossed Faolan's face, as he stepped backward. His friend was acting in a very odd manner. "You don't look well."

For a moment, Cathal was taken back. A suppressed part of his mind understood that he was acting in an irrational manner, but for the life of him, he couldn't care less. The poison that permeated his addled mind compelled him onward, quelling all rational doubt. "I've never felt better," he assured his friend. "In a couple of days, the curse will be lifted. Birka will once again be under the protection of the old gods, as it should be."

Faolan narrowed his eyes and canted his head to the side; his finer Christian sensibilities taking hold of him. His initial reaction was to lash out and condemn the blasphemous monument, but instead he simply shook his head and said, "I don't understand."

With an assured smile, Cathal replied, "I will tell you the same thing I told the chieftain: I am certain the Slavic god Veles is responsible for the evil behind these wolf attacks. And who is the mortal enemy of Veles? Perun, god of thunder! You see, not only do the Norse, Slavic, and Celtic religions acknowledge werewolves, but they each have a god of thunder. Thor is the Norse god of Thunder, Perun is the Slavic god of thunder, and Taranis is the Celtic god of thunder! I have supplicated Taranis for his wisdom, and he has shown me the way. To purge this town of corruption, we must construct a giant wicker man, made of wood and packed with humans, to sacrifice to the gods. Only then shall the ancient ones deliver us from evil!"

Shaking his head, Faolan held up his hands and said, "Are you even listening to yourself? That sounds like complete madness!"

Cathal leveled his gaze at his friend and said without a hint of equivocation, "Sanity is a small price to pay for the favor of the gods. *You* of all people should understand."

"What do you mean?" asked Faolan.

"Back in Ireland...haven't you heard of the legend of St. Patrick and the werewolves?"

Shaking his head, Faolan said, "Maybe...when I was a boy. What are you getting at?"

"Five hundred years ago, when St. Patrick came to Ireland, he was incensed that certain tribes refused to convert to Christianity, so he cursed them, turning the supposed heretics into werewolves."

"What does *that* have to do with anything?"

"Isn't it obvious? There's nothing in the Christian doctrine that would have given St. Peter the knowledge or power to do such a thing. It was the druids that instructed St. Peter in such matters."

Faolan shook his head, uncomprehending.

"St. Peter took the ancient knowledge of the druids and used it to suit his own needs, without the concession of the Celtic gods-"

"Stop! Just...stop it. You are making a mockery of Christianity, twisting these fables, and that's what they are, *fables*, to suit your own convoluted needs. I mean, just look at you!"

"Faolan, I-"

The Irishman held up his hands, interrupting Cathal once again. "I want no part of this – whatever *this* is. I simply came down here to tell you that Torsten arrested Domyan and Danika. They're both in holding cells in Birka, awaiting trial."

"What? He can't do that without any evidence."

"Apparently, he has witnesses." Faolan stared at the giant legs of the effigy, then shook his head in exasperation. "I fear for your safety. What if, after you sacrifice all those Norsemen, nothing happens? They'll crucify you."

"Don't distress yourself over such matters. Taranis has a plan."

With a heavy sigh, Faolan turned around and walked back to the lumber camp. He knew that his friend was beyond reason.

"Faolan, stay! There's nothing for you back at the lumber camp. With Domyan locked up, how will you be paid?"

As he walked away, the Irishman briefly turned his head and replied, "I won't be a part of this madness. I hope you come to your senses before it's too late."

Cathal sat by the hearth, staring into the flames. He was pleased with the day's progress. Both legs of the effigy were constructed, and the laborers were currently working on the torso. Cathal insisted they work in shifts, and work diligently through the night. It was the only way the statue would be completed in time for the ritual. They had a span of three days, where the full moon would be shining overhead.

It was late in the evening, and the chieftain had just tucked his daughter into bed. Torsten wandered aimlessly about the longhouse, drinking mead and mumbling curses under his breath. The responsibilities of leadership never seemed to end, he lamented.

Cathal watched the chieftain for a time, then finally asked, "What evidence do you have against Domyan and his sister?"

Torsten barked out a short laugh and said, "What evidence do I need? We recently came under one of the worst attacks in this town's history. I'm simply mitigating the chance of another attack."

"But surely you can't just imprison someone without a trial. There are laws..."

"Those laws are for Norsemen!" shouted Torsten, as he pointed an accusing finger at Cathal. He then composed himself and said, "Of course there will be a trial. In a couple of days, during the ritual sacrifice to the gods, Domyan and Danika will be brought before the judges. *They* will determine if the foreman and his sister are innocent or not."

Judges? Cathal understood only the rudiments of Norse law. The judges in Norse society were people of high station, respected and venerated, but they were *not* impartial. No doubt they would look unfavorably upon the Slavs. He scowled; Cathal didn't care what happened to Domyan, he was sure the foreman was guilty of *something,* but his sister...

The fringes of Cathal's muddled mind twisted and pulled at his sanity. He held his fingers to his temples and rubbed in a measured, circular motion. Would he simply stand by while his beloved was unjustly accused?

He let out a sharp laugh. *Beloved*? Since when did he think of Danika in that manner? He must be more unbalanced than he initially thought.

"Eh? What's so amusing?" asked Torsten.

"Nothing. Everything," answered Cathal, as he continued to stare into the flames of the hearth.

From behind him, Cathal heard the chieftain mutter another curse, then he heard a muffled thump, as Torsten crashed into his bed. Soon, loud drunken snores reverberated throughout the longhouse.

With an exasperated exhale, Cathal stood up and paced the dirt floor of the main room, shaking his head. His frustrations mounted with each step; he *had* to see her. He shot a furtive glance towards the chieftain's bedroom, he then quietly opened the front door of the longhouse and escaped into the night.

"Where are you going?" asked the guardsman stationed outside the door.

"Where do you think? I'm checking on the statue's progress," lied Cathal, as he stomped down the dark trail. After he was out of the guard's sight, he turned to his left and walked towards the prison cells – a series of small wooden structures used to house criminals awaiting trial.

Luckily, Torsten informed his guardsmen that Cathal had full authority, and they were to comply with all his requests relating to the ritual and the effigy. As Cathal approached the prison cells, he asked the guardsmen which cell housed the female Slav. He was quickly directed to a small, dark, windowless cabin.

After instructing the guardsman to wait ten paces from the holding cell, Cathal walked into the pitch-black room and closed the door behind him. For a moment, he was gripped with fear. He then cursed his love-struck stupidity. What if Danika was a...

"I recognized your voice," said Danika, as she sat up in her cot.

Cathal squinted his eyes, straining to see through the darkness. "Are they treating you well?" he asked.

"As well as could be expected."

With his hands held out before him, Cathal found the edge of her cot and sat down beside her. He felt more than a little awkward. He wanted to say so much to her, yet he could not find the right words. Finally, he said, "I'm sorry. I had no idea Torsten was planning to have you and your brother arrested. I didn't find out until Faolan informed me just a few hours ago."

"There's nothing you could have done," lamented Danika. "The chieftain has despised us since the day we arrived in Birka. He's been looking for an excuse to lock us away."

"Still, it's not right. Hell, I don't think it's even legal." Cathal shook his head, unsure of what to do or say. Finally, he said, "What do you think will happen to you?"

"Banishment, if we're lucky. But I don't think we'll be so fortunate. The people of Birka need closure, and it seems that my brother and I are going to be the victims for their groundless accusations."

Cathal let out a heavy sigh and said, "I figured as much." He then stood up and walked to the door. He opened the door slightly and peered through the crack, then quietly closed it. "I can get you out of here. I'll distract the guards, and you can make your escape-"

"To what end?" she interrupted. "We're on a small island; trapped. There's simply nowhere to run."

He walked back towards her and sat down. If only he could see her dark brown eyes; her beautiful blond hair. "I wish things could have been different between us. I'm not ashamed to admit that I've thought about you often." Cathal caught himself, afraid he might say too much. His muddled state of mind granted him moments of dreadful confusion and moments of great clarity. He wasn't even sure if his feelings for her were real or not. He cursed himself inwardly; if only he had more time.

She placed her hand on his knee and said, "In another life, perhaps."

Cathal placed his hand over hers and choked back a sob that stubbornly rose in his throat. "Yes, in another life."

As he stood up, he felt her hand fall away from his knee. He clenched his jaw and stepped forward. Before he reached for the door, he said, "How long did you know about Mirko?"

Her voice sounded distant and full of regret. "I knew about him from the very beginning."

"And your brother, is he one of them?"

Silence.

After waiting for a moment, he quietly opened the door and stepped outside. A warm summer breeze washed over him. He could smell the salty air from the ocean. Looking to his left, he could see the small windowless cell where Domyan was being held. Cathal furrowed his brow. If Domyan could turn into the same creature as Mirko, then he could easily break out of his cell. So why didn't he?

With measured steps, he approached Domyan's cell, then stopped. There was nothing to be gained from talking to the man. Cathal knew that Domyan would never give up his secrets, and yet the council expected him to procure as much information as possible for their chronicles. Shaking his head, he stepped forward and waved the guardsman away. Then, reaching for the door handle, he froze.

"Just a moment," he told the guardsman. "Have your weapon ready."

The guardsman grabbed his ax and rested the haft of the weapon casually on his shoulder, unaware of the danger present.

Cathal let out a short, agitated snort. Steeling his nerves, he opened the door. Moonlight washed into the small room, revealing a man who was standing just beyond the door. The light only came up to his shoulders, leaving his face veiled in darkness.

"You've been talking to my sister," said Domyan in a listless tone.

"I simply wanted to know her side of the story."

"I'll bet," he laughed. "So tell me the truth. Were you working for the chieftain all this time?"

"What?"

"Heh. For a doctor, you aren't that smart. I had my suspicions about you the moment you walked into my camp. I figured the chieftain would hire someone from the outside; someone who wasn't a Norseman to come and spy on me."

"No. I can assure you that I'm a doctor from Ireland." Cathal then stiffened, as he heard a sniffing noise coming from the foreman.

"You smell that?" said Domyan in a low whisper.

"I...what?" Cathal could see moonlight glinting off the foreman's teeth.

"Lies. Do you smell the lies?"

Suddenly, Cathal felt as if he were clutched in ice. His pupils shrunk to pinpoints as his distraught mind saw inky monstrosities reaching out from the darkness, towards his petrified soul. He stumbled back a step, then slammed the door shut, as Domyan laughed a banshees laugh.

"You think this is a game, Irishman? You think you can come into my camp, steal my secrets, and fuck my sister? You know nothing!" he screamed.

Crack! The thick oaken door bulged outward for a second as Domyan slammed against it. He then started to pound on the door with his bare hands. "You'll be the last to die, Irishman! I'm saving you for last!"

Cathal tripped over his feet and fell backwards. He then lurched forward and stumbled down the dark path towards Birka, as Domyan continued to scream and pound on the door from inside his cell.

Chapter 16

The next morning, Cathal woke up to the sound of hammering and sawing. He was in the chieftain's longhouse, curled up in the corner of the main room, sleeping on the dirt floor with a few inches of straw scattered beneath him for padding. As he pushed his way to a sitting position, he gazed out the window. From the position of the sun, it appeared to be late morning.

With a yawn, he tossed aside the woolen blanket that was covering him. He then stretched and slowly wiped the sleep from his eyes. Clutching his head, he muttered a few curses; he wasn't sure if the hammering was coming from the construction site or from inside his head.

That reminded him – it was time to take his daily dose of poison. He took the small vial from one of the pouches cinched to his belt and held it before him. His stomach involuntarily heaved as he looked at the greenish-black mixture. Shaking his head in consternation, he uncorked the small vial and carefully took a sip, shuddering as the liquid burned its way down his throat.

He clenched his eyes shut, then opened them, almost certain that he saw strange tentacles lash and sway from the corners of his distorted visage. The hallucinations were getting worse, but he contented himself with the fact that, for better or worse, it would soon be over – the curse would either be lifted from this island or he would soon be dead.

The guardsman opened the front door of the longhouse and stepped inside. He looked around for a moment, then spied Cathal sitting on the floor. Then, with pursed lips and an arrogant countenance, he said, "The chieftain wants to talk to you, down by the construction site."

Cathal nodded in acknowledgment and slowly climbed to his feet, more than a little unsteady. He then pulled on his boots and walked through the door, as the guardsman eyed him with suspicion.

Ignoring the Norseman, Cathal trudged down the dirt path towards the construction site. As the sound of hammering grew louder, the pain inside his head pulsed and pounded.

"It's about damn time you woke up," yelled Torsten. He was standing next to the effigy, beckoning to him with one hand.

As Cathal approached the giant statue, he craned his head upward. The workers had bound and nailed the giant wicker torso to the legs – the monument already stood twenty feet at the shoulder, and the head wasn't even attached yet.

"One day ahead of schedule!" beamed Torsten. "In less than twelve hours, the effigy will be complete. We will make the sacrifice to the gods tonight, and by tomorrow morning, the curse will be lifted."

So soon? Surprised though he was, the jabbering voices in his mind kept him distracted. "Yes," whispered Cathal, rubbing his temple with one hand.

The chieftain narrowed his eyes suspiciously. "You're not having second thoughts, are you? If the workers suspect you of going back on your word, there will be hell to pay."

"No, absolutely not," assured Cathal, looking up with focused eyes. "It's just that...the preparations have taken a lot out of me. Make no mistake, I'll be ready." Cathal attempted to sound more confident than he actually was.

"Good. The last thing I need is a riot. The people of this town are so wound up that almost no one has bothered with going to work today." The chieftain then exhaled loudly and said, "The sooner this mess is over with, the better."

Cathal looked to the side of the statue, where the workers were constructing the wooden head and arms, yet to be attached. The colossal wicker head seemed to be staring at him with accusing eyes. Cathal averted his gaze and said, "Why is Danika a suspect in the murders? All of the werewolves that were spotted had black fur, yet she has blond hair."

"Eh? What are you talking about?"

"It makes sense, doesn't it? If a person changes into a beast, why would the color of their hair change? Danika has blond hair, yet no one has seen a werewolf with that color of fur."

The chieftain scratched at his beard and furrowed his brow. "You might have a point," he admitted. "But there are two creatures that must be accounted for. If the people of Birka see only one man on trial tonight, there will be an uprising."

"But the judges will surely absolve her of all charges, once they hear the evidence, and we'll be in the same predicament."

"Dammit!" grumbled Torsten. "Blast it all to hell. Why must this be so difficult? Fine, I'll have my guardsmen round up the rest of the Slavs. We'll keep them imprisoned until we get this mess settled."

"You can't just imprison-"

"That's final!" the chieftain interrupted. "You haven't seen the panic in the villager's eyes. You've been mulling around doing god knows what, while I've been doing all the work around here – overseeing the construction of this...thing. I'm trying to run this town and what have you done? You just sit in my longhouse and jabber nonsense to yourself all day long. Nine hells, this entire island has gone mad." With that, the chieftain turned around and stomped off towards the tavern.

Cathal watched after him for a moment, then he turned his head and looked at the docks, not a hundred yards away. A part of him wanted to steal a boat and be rid of this place; this insanity. He let out a bitter sigh and walked around the giant monument, inspecting its progress.

As he oversaw the construction of the giant statue, he obsessed over the possibility of a third werewolf. After the death of Mirko, there were rumors of two more of the beasts. He was fairly certain that Domyan was one, but he had no idea who the other lycanthrope could possibly be. Most of the Norsemen in Birka had light-colored hair. *Most,* not all. There were a half-dozen Slavs back at the logging camp, most of whom had black hair, and *all* the Turks at the reindeer camp had black hair. Cathal almost laughed in exasperation. Perhaps the chieftain had the right idea – imprison anyone even slightly suspect.

Dusk came all too quickly. As the sun set to the west, casting looming shadows over the bleak island. The ponderous moon inched its way ever upward. To the north, he saw a solemn procession of Norsemen walking their way towards the effigy. It didn't take long to figure out who they were – the injured hunters from the infirmary, escorted by a few guardsmen. They stopped at the base of the giant statue.

Cathal watched in silence as the doomed Norsemen were packed into the wicker man. To their credit, they did not complain nor attempt to run. Peering closer, it seemed as if the men, who were infected with the frothing disease, were drunk beyond measure. *Good*, he thought. *The alcohol will cause them to burn faster.*

A slightly hysterical laugh escaped him, attracting a few worried glances from the laborers. They were more than a little apprehensive of him, as Cathal had been jabbering away to himself throughout most of the day. It took nearly all his will to maintain a marginally sane countenance.

He cocked his head back and gazed at the ominous wicker man. The effigy was completely built. It stood twenty-four feet tall, and was packed with eighteen sacrificial victims. They were packed in tightly, with no room to move, with no chance to escape.

The villagers started gathering around the wicker man. They arrived in two's and three's, gawking and pointing their fingers at the giant effigy. They formed a half-circle, with Cathal between them and the statue. To his side were two thick wooden posts, sticking four feet out of the ground. Cathal narrowed his eyes, wondering what they were for.

Then, from the direction of the prison cells, Cathal could see several guardsmen escorting Domyan. The foreman was staring at him with an almost amused expression.

Cathal cautiously stepped back, as the guards led the accused to the wooden posts. They shackled the foreman's wrists to each post with iron chains. *Ah, so that's what they're for*, he thought.

Domyan looked over the gathering crowd with an air of thinly-veiled disgust. He then casually glanced upward, towards the full moon, then shifted his gaze to Cathal, with a smirk creasing his face.

Nervously stepping away, Cathal walked around to the back of the effigy, keeping the giant wicker foot between him and the foreman. He did not want Domyan to see the fear that was permeating from his very pores. "Taranis, give me strength," he whispered to himself, as he touched the foot of the statue. The sheer size and ominous presence of the effigy fortified his determination.

"We're all set then?" said a familiar voice behind him.

Cathal stiffly turned around and nodded. "It's perfect," he affirmed, with an ardent glint in his eyes.

The chieftain nodded and placed his hand on Cathal's shoulder. "Good. The sooner we get this over with, the better. In a few moments, my guardsmen will light the effigy. As it starts to burn, I want you to say a few words to the villagers. Something inspiring. I'm also going to have the Christian priest say a few words." Torsten then motioned to his left, where a bald man in a black robe was apprehensively standing, shifting his weight from foot to foot.

The priest nervously nodded towards Cathal, who nodded back in silence.

"Alright, then," continued Torsten. "After the speeches are given, and the sacrifices have been made, the judges will discuss the fate of Domyan and his sister. When they judge them guilty, gods willing, we'll be done with this mess."

Guilty? Did Torsten know something that Cathal did not? He narrowed his eyes in suspicion, but decided not to pursue the matter. He then looked over the multitude of unfamiliar faces. Where was Danika? After scanning the crowd for a few moments, he finally spotted her – she was surrounded by a group of stern guardsmen, two of which were holding her by the arms. She briefly met his gaze, then looked downward in apathy, her blond hair falling over her face.

A few moments later, and all was ready. Torsten lifted his hand, signaling for the proceedings to begin. Two guardsmen carrying torches walked around the giant wicker man and started to light the effigy. As the flames climbed up the legs of the statue, the condemned Norsemen trapped inside started to sing a melancholy dirge. A few of the men who were closest to the flames started to weep and wail, begging Odin to deliver them. The chieftain then turned his head and offered

Cathal a curt nod, motioning for him to begin his speech.

Cathal slowly walked to the front of the burning effigy. To his right was Domyan. The foreman was looking at him in a vindictive manner, sneering in utter disdain. Cathal tried his best to ignore him. Raising his hands in the air, he asked the crowd for their attention. The villagers, nearly five hundred of them, nervously eyed the druid, unsure of what to expect.

After clearing his throat, Cathal said, "For as long as we have been on this earth, we have had a deep connection with the wolf. When the gods created humanity and placed us on this earth, the animals were already here, living in balance with nature, but the humans upset that balance. We upset the balance of nature with no care or consequence, and for that, we have been judged.

"With our bows and axes, we've been able to distance ourselves from the horrors of predation. We have been able to distance ourselves from that ancient, eternal hunger, and that in itself has made us weak. We thrive in the safety of our modern trappings, without a care to the horrors that lie in the woods that surround us.

"We do not belong in nature. Our pale bodies hold no part in the natural cycle of this world. Take for instance the balance between predator and prey – where is *our* place in this cycle? Man kills the animals, cuts down the trees, and mines the very minerals from this earth, and what do we give back? Nothing.

"I tell you there is a dark side to nature, a side that rights the blasphemies against itself with terrible vengeance. In our hubris, we have even taken the wolf, and domesticated the animal to our own needs. Did you think that you could just take from those predators without giving back? Did you think your could rape this land of its trees and ore and animals without consequence?

"The gods have seen your greed and judged you guilty. That is why the dark gods have risen up and cursed this land, and that is why we have constructed this terrible effigy and offer these sacrifices – to appease the old gods and beg their forgiveness. As these noble men burn for our sins, I ask you to pray to your chosen gods. Ask them to deliver us from our avarice. For it is when we destroy this land around us, we destroy ourselves, and for that I humbly ask the gods for forgiveness."

The crowd of villagers remained silent. There was but a mere inkling of understanding as to what the druid was recounting, but they did understand one thing – that they were paying the consequences for their greed. Whether Norse or Slavic or Christian, they were all guilty.

Cathal slowly stepped back and nodded to the Christian priest, who stepped forward with a look of righteous indignation.

The priest raised his hand and pointed to the effigy and yelled, "This is blasphemy! It is an affront to the one true god!"

A wailing laugh erupted from Domyan. There was an insidious look in the foreman's eyes as he yelled, "You think this will appease the gods? They laugh at your pathetic grasp of the *true* nature of this world! Now you will see what happens when you take that which is not yours. Now you shall see the true power of Veles!"

Domyan's eyes began to turn a dark amber as he wrenched and twisted at the chains that bound him.

"This man is guilty of worshiping a false god!" accused the priest. He then turned and pointed at the crowd and said, "And *you* are all guilty of taking part in this sacrilege!"

A maniacal laugh interrupted the clergyman. "You die first, priest!" shouted Domyan as he yanked on his chains. "You will die, then that pathetic excuse of a chieftain will die, and then you, Cathal." The foreman whipped his head around and looked straight at the druid. There was something about Domyan's countenance, something changing...

It was then that Cathal heard the sound of a terrible howling emanating from the forest, as what sounded like a throng of wolves cried out into the night. Then, from all around him, wolves by the hundreds raced out of the surrounding woods, towards the villagers. As the impending horror approached, Cathal's mind, in a vain attempt to protect his sanity, shut off for a moment – he could neither hear nor see, as everything around him transformed into a muted blackness. Then slowly, the ghastly sights and sounds around him came into focus. He could hear the roaring flames of the effigy, the screams of the sacrificial victims, the excited yipping of hungry wolves, and Domyan's demonic laughter.

The wolves ran towards the villagers in carefully coordinated attack patterns, honed by eons of instinct and aggression. The malicious predators were bent on killing every last one of the villagers. It was no contest; the wolves were much stronger and quicker than their pale, nearly defenseless victims.

The villagers, eyes wide with panic, tried in vain to escape, but they had no weapons to protect themselves! They were brought down by the dozens. The wolves bit and gnashed over the frightened villagers, dragging them into the forest, or feasting upon their bodies where they lie, as the victims screamed for mercy.

Then Cathal, momentarily distracted by the carnage surrounding him, watched in awe as Domyan started to change. Among the chaos and pandemonium of the wolf attacks, the foreman screamed as his forearms and cheeks started to sprout coarse, black hair. He then crouched down, as his legs contorted and his heels elongated, ripping his pants and boots away. His shoulders quivered and buckled and burst through the fabric of his tunic – powerful, contorted muscles rippled and broadened to frightening size.

Cathal screamed for the guardsmen to kill Domyan, but they were too busy trying to protect the populace from the wolf attacks.

With an effortless shrug of its mighty shoulders, the werewolf broke the shackles that bound it. There was no trace of Domyan left in the beast, only pure, unbridled hatred and rage. The beast turned and approached the druid with a malicious snort.

The priest then stepped forward. He was standing between Cathal and the werewolf, with a look of righteous indignation in his eyes. He raised his crucifix before him and yelled, "The power of Christ compels yoAAAAaaarrrrgggh!" His scream was cut short as the werewolf raised it's clawed hand, and with a mighty swipe tore the priest nearly in half. Blood sprayed into the night air, staining the earth with red and gore.

Lifting its head towards the moon, the werewolf let out a bloodcurdling roar. Its eyes were crazed beyond measure, reflecting a symphony of malevolence.

The hundreds of wolves that surrounded them, savagely attacked with practiced ease. They tore into the villagers and guardsmen, snapping and gnashing and killing. And amongst it all, the werewolf stepped towards Cathal, enjoying the fear in the druid's piteous eyes.

"Face me, demon," yelled Torsten, as he charged towards the werewolf, hefting a giant battleaxe. With an intense grimace contorting his face, the chieftain swung his blade at the monster with all his might.

The werewolf effortlessly grabbed the haft of the weapon with one clawed hand, instantly stopping the momentum of the chieftain's attack. It then opened its great maw and clamped down on Torsten's head, crushing it like a ripe melon. As the chieftain went limp, the werewolf chomped and chewed, and after a few grizzly bites, swallowed Torsten's severed head.

As the werewolf was distracted, feasting on the remains of the chieftain, Cathal looked wildly around him. To his left, he saw a discarded bow and a quiver of arrows lying next to a dead guardsman. He stepped forward as quickly as he could, yet it seemed as if he were moving through a twisted dream, mired in quicksand.

Finally, he reached down and grabbed one of the arrows from the guard's quiver. Then, quickly as he could, he opened his pouch of wolfsbane and dipped the tip of the arrow into the pouch. With the speed of desperation,

Cathal grabbed the bow off the ground and notched the arrow.

Looking up, he could see the werewolf approach him, an insidious grin etched on its repulsive face. Cathal whispered, "Taranis, guide my shot," as he pulled back on the drawstring and let the arrow loose.

The arrow shot straight towards the werewolf's heart, yet the beast was so fast that it lurched away from the projectile at the last instant, causing the arrow to miss by a fraction of an inch. A triumphant look glinted across the creature's malevolent eyes as it lunged towards Cathal with blinding speed.

Before Cathal could react, the werewolf was upon him, sinking its powerful jaws into his shoulder, with the intent of ripping him limb from limb. But as the creature's sharp teeth sunk deeper into his flesh, Cathal's blood seeped into the beast's mouth, absorbing into its bloodstream.

The beast's pupils shrunk to mere pinpoints, as its eyes widened in absolute shock. The werewolf then released its grip and staggered backwards, as the poison that coursed through Cathal's veins transferred into its own. The creature shook and convulsed, then started to wretch, trying to expel the poison from its body. As the werewolf vomited, the skull and brains of Torsten spewed over the hapless druid, who was lying on the ground, covering his face with his arms.

Cathal recoiled in horror as he was bathed in the wet, putrid remains of the chieftain. Looking down at his chest, he could see a portion of Torsten's face stuck to his tunic, with the chieftain's baleful eye looking straight at him. With terrified apprehension, he brushed the bloody gristle off his chest and madly crawled backwards, away from the convulsing beast.

Everywhere he looked was complete pandemonium; the wolves were ripping the villagers apart in a mad display of unbridled aggression. He watched in dismay as a few surviving villagers tried to run into the forest, only to be chased and savagely brought down by the ravenous predators. Despite the horror that surrounded him, Cathal was incredulous as to why none of the wolves attacked him.

The werewolf was now on its knees, twitching and convulsing, trying in vain to expel the poison from its body. Blood streamed from its nose and maw as it shook its giant head back and forth. Then, the beast shuddered and looked directly towards Cathal. It strained through its vocal cords, but was unable to form the proper words.

How? It seemed to ask.

Cathal gazed into the beast's hateful eyes and muttered, "It was my own cowardice. I knew there was no way I could stop you from killing me, so I increased my tolerance to wolfsbane, thinking that if you killed me, I would take you with me. I had no idea the poison would work so fast."

The beast stared at him for a moment, then closed its eyes. It then convulsed and lurched over the ground, seemingly reaching for something just beyond the trees in the distance. It then rolled over onto its back and gazed up at the night sky, its eyes fixated on the full moon overhead. With one final shudder, the werewolf let out a final gasp and went limp.

The instant the werewolf expired, the maddened wolves ceased their attack. They looked around in bewilderment, as if they had just woken from a dream. The wolves ignored their hapless prey and simply loped back into the forest, as if beckoned.

Cathal watched after the wolves for a moment, squinting his eyes through the thick smoke that was billowing from the effigy. The giant wicker man was now all but burnt away, with the charred, blackened bodies of eighteen sacrificial victims lying motionless on the ground. He then shifted his gaze and looked out over the field – now a bloody battleground littered with broken, dying bodies. There was nary a survivor amongst the hundreds of villagers.

The town of Birka was completely lost.

Through the dense smoke that lay over the rolling countryside, Cathal saw movement not a hundred feet away. From the forest, a figure walked slowly towards him. It seemed to glide through the blackened clouds of smoke. The wolves yipped and danced around the creature as it approached. Cathal watched in mounting horror as the beast stepped closer. A few moments later, a gentle breeze washed the smoke away, revealing a woman with blond hair, looking at him with sorrow in her eyes.

Cathal gazed at her in disbelief, caught in the disparity of her beauty against the grizzly horror of the battlefield she tread upon. "How?" he asked, choking down his anguish.

Danika looked into his eyes with mournful regret. Then, slowly reaching her hand to the top of her head, she curled her fingers around her hair and pulled off the blond wig, revealing shortly-cropped black hair. She stood there, wrapped in misery, as the wig dropped to the ground. "I'm so sorry," she said, as tears streamed down her cheeks. "I'm so sorry." She then turned and slowly walked back towards the forest, and was soon lost behind a cloud of acrid black smoke, with the wolves following closely behind her.

Cathal was left with nothing but his own emptiness and remorse. He lowered his gaze and looked at the still form of Domyan. The foreman's dead eyes were staring upward at the pale moon.

The Irishman then slowly shook his head. Domyan took his sanity, and Danika took his heart. And while his mind would recover from the ravages of wolfsbane poisoning, he knew that his heart would forever be under the thrall of Danika's shadow.

He simply sat there, lost and embittered. He knew the only reason the wolves didn't attack him, was because Danika willed it to be so. Cathal then reached up and grasped the bite wound on his shoulder. Was he infected by Domyan's bite, or would the wolfsbane protect him from the contagion? He lowered his head in utter despondency; he did not care.

From the fringes of the smoky landscape, he saw two figures running towards him. One of the figures was human, bent over and gasping for air. The other figure was a wolf, chasing after the unfortunate man. Cathal then squinted his eyes and craned his head forward. No, it wasn't a wolf at all, he realized. It was Biter and Faolan!

Faolan had a bewildered grin on his face, as he coughed and wheezed, trying to catch his breath in the smoky air. "I can't believe you're alive!" he coughed. He then looked wildly around him, more than a little apprehensive. "We need to get out of here." He reached out his hand, which Cathal accepted, and pulled him to his feet.

The two Irishmen staggered through the black smoke towards the docks, where several fishing boats lie moored. As the three climbed into the nearest boat, Faolan grabbed the oars, while Cathal sat at the aft of the boat, cradling his arm.

"Are you going to be alright?" asked Faolan as he started to row out to sea. He seemed to be following the coastline to the mainland.

With an exasperated smile, Cathal nodded his head. "I'll be fine. I can't believe that *you* of all people made it through that madness. What are the odds that out of all the hundreds of people on the island, we would be the only survivors?"

As he rowed, Faolan engendered a thoughtful look, but said nothing.

"I must say, when I first arrived at the logging camp, I thought you were the werewolf," admitted Cathal.

"Why would you say that?"

Cathal slowly exhaled, then said, "It didn't make sense that the Slavs would kill their own people. Why would Domyan and Mirko kill those closest to them, instead of the other migrants or Norsemen?"

Faolan considered Cathal's words, then asked, "Why *would* Domyan kill his own kind?"

Cathal squinted his eyes thoughtfully and said, "I think each one of us has a beast inside – some raw, savage force that lives to hunt and kill. We try to suppress that instinct and live our lives as civilized people, but that rage is always there, simmering just below the surface. I can only speculate, but I believe the werewolf hates the human part of itself. I think the werewolf hates all of humanity, no matter the race or gender. When someone changes into that beast, all civilized restraint is gone, they simply lash out and harm those closest to them." He then shook his head and repeated, "I simply can't believe that *you* of all people made it through that madness."

Faolan continued to row in silence for a few moments. Then, canting his head to the side, he asked, "Do you remember when, after you killed Mirko, you asked me if I was bitten?"

"Yes. Why?"

Faolan stared directly at him. The moonlight was glinting off his amber eyes. "Well...I might have lied," he said, with a wolfish grin.

The End.

After/words

History / Characters / Ending

The History

The first mythological reference of a man turning into a wolf was written in 1550 BC. King Lycaon of Arcadia tried to trick Zeus, father of the Greek gods. Zeus, furious at the attempt to deceive him, turned Lycaon into a wolf. This is where the term lycanthropy comes from.

The idea for *Shadow of the Werewolf* came from reading the Völsunga saga – an Icelandic saga written in the 13th century. In one part of the story, two men by the name of Sigmund and Sinfjotli broke into a house where they found a couple of magical wolf skins. When they wore the skins, they were transformed into wolves.

In researching the different cultures and mythologies for this book, I was very surprised to find that most of the different mythologies I studied had their own narrative on werewolf lore, whether they be Celtic, Greek, Norse, Turkish, or Slavic. Those comparative mythologies became central to the story of *Shadow of the Werewolf*.

The frothing disease was, of course, rabies. Incubation time for the disease is generally one to three months. However, to heighten the tension of this story, I had this particular strain affect its victims more quickly; within a week. Rabies was first documented 4000 years ago in the *Codex of Eshnunna*, a Mesopotamian text from 1930 BC.

The town of Birka was an actual settlement during the Viking Age. The town was located on the island of Björkö, which is eighteen miles west of Stockholm, Sweden. In the book,

I made the island of Björkö larger, in order to accommodate so many wolves. *Shadow of the Werewolf* takes place in 950AD, roughly the same year the historical town of Birka was abandoned.

The Characters

The protagonist for *Shadow of the Werewolf* needed to be someone who understood the history and mythology of different cultures, which is something the average Norseman simply didn't concern himself with. The main character needed to be an outsider – a studious man who could connect the similarities between different histories and mythologies. That's when I came up with the concept of the druids investigating different curiosities across the known world.

While the druids were mentioned a few times by Greek and Roman scholars, including Julius Caesar himself, very little is known about them. The druids maintained all of their history, mythology, laws and poetry in an oral tradition; they simply didn't keep any of it written down. This became another plot point for *Shadow of the Werewolf*, as Cathal is studying to become a full druid, which takes twenty years to learn the oral traditions. In the meantime, the council of druids sent him on various missions to prove his worth.

For the antagonist(s) of the story, I wanted to approach those characters as an antithesis of the main character – instead of studious and contemplative, I wanted Domyan and Mirko to be close-minded, suspicious, and brutish men. In addition, Domyan had a manic-depressive personality; sometimes he was friendly, but most of the time he was not. This dual nature reflected his human/beast dichotomy. On the other hand, Danika was a victim of her curse. She asked Cathal about exorcism, only for the clueless druid to misunderstand the importance of her question. Danika was torn between the loyalty for her brother, and her love for Cathal.

The Ending

The ultimate goal of *Shadow of the Werewolf,* was to study the psychological contention between man vs. myth, man vs. nature, and man vs. himself.

The story also has an ecological theme. I wanted to impress upon the reader that taking from nature has consequences. This is represented by the industry of Birka – the loggers, the herders, the fishermen and the miners are all taking from the land without care to sustainability. What they don't realize is that nature eventually strikes back, often with deadly results.

While two of the three werewolves died by the end of the story, I wanted Danika to represent a different facet of the werewolf curse – that of an unwilling and sympathetic character. While Domyan and Mirko embraced their wolfish nature, Danika was at odds with her condition. And while she couldn't bring herself to oppose her brother, she used her power over the wolves to protect Cathal during the final wolf attack. But in the end, she knew that because of her curse, she could never have a normal relationship. She walks back into the forest alone, despite the fact that Cathal is still madly in love with her. This is where the title, *Shadow of the Werewolf*, comes from – while Cathal can never be with her, his heart will forever be under her shadow.

The final scene of the story is a classic standoff. Faolan reveals that he is a werewolf, but it is unknown if he can change at will, or if the change comes upon him involuntarily. If he changes into a werewolf and bites Cathal, he will die from wolfsbane poisoning, but as a werewolf, would he even have the rationality to stop himself from such an action? It is also unknown if Cathal himself is a werewolf, or if the wolfsbane protected him from the contagion. I think leaving the story on such a precipitous note, pays homage to the doomed nature of many classic horror novels, such as those written by H.P. Lovecraft.

The V for Viking Saga

I hope you enjoyed my tale of werewolves, druids, and dark gods. If you would like to read more about the Viking Age, I happen to have a series of books on the very subject. The 'V for Viking' Saga is a series of character-driven stories that focus on Viking society and personal struggles. Each book is a complete stand-alone novel that uses the same supporting characters and locations. However, the books are also written in chronological order, for those who want to experience the full five-book saga.

If you're in the mood for more psychological/wolfish horror, I highly recommend *Vision of the Viking*. It's the story of a Norse seeress who struggles with her own encroaching madness.

The 'V for Viking' Saga includes:

C= Characters

The Vikings:

Book 1 - Vengeance of the Viking

- The story of a Viking hunter and his pet bear.

- C: Torleif, Viggo, Gunnar, Chubbers the bear (30-300 pounds)

Book 2 - Valor of the Viking

- A skald (Viking musician) joins the criminal underground.

- C: Randulf, Torleif, Modoc, Viggo, Chubbers the bear (300 pounds)

Book 3 - Valley of the Viking

- Germanic barbarians lay siege to a Viking settlement.

- C: Buma, Torleif, Modoc, Viggo, Randulf, Chubbers the bear (400 pounds)

The Viking Seeress:

Book 1 - Vision of the Viking

- A Viking seeress must deal with the aftermath of a devastating siege, while struggling with her own encroaching madness.

- C: Brenna, Buma, Torleif, Viggo, Chubbers the bear (600 pounds)

Book 2 - Vendetta of the Viking

- Two treacherous murderers overthrow a Viking settlement.

- C: Brenna, Torleif, Dagny, Randulf, Viggo, Chubbers (700 pounds)

Also by Magnus Hansen:

The Last Varangian – Just released!

980 AD: A doomed castle is surrounded by enemy soldiers. The king offers a mountain of silver to any mercenary army who would help defend against imminent attack. But who would be insane enough to agree to such a suicide mission?

Why, the Varangians, of course...

* * * * * * *

Author's website:

AuthorMagnusHansen.wordpress.com

If you would like to send the author an email, he can be reached at:

MagnusHansen300@gmail.com

And lastly, I have one small request: If you enjoyed this book, I would be very grateful if you could take a moment and leave a review on Amazon, even if it's only a few words.

Printed in Great Britain
by Amazon